i

imaginist

the
Book
of
Books

想象另一种可能

理
想
国
imaginist

THE
UNCOMMON
READER

—— Alan Bennett ——

非普通读者

[英] 艾伦·贝内特 著

何 宁 译

广西师范大学出版社
·桂林·

You don't put your life into your books.
You find it there.

夜晚的温莎城堡中，正在举行国宴。宾主正慢步走向滑铁卢厅，女王与法国总统在前，王室成员殿后。

　　"现在我可以和你单独说会儿话了。"女王对总统说。她边说边向左右微笑致意，周围一片衣香鬓影，冠盖云集。"我想和你讨论一下让·热内[1]这位作家。"

　　"哦，"总统答道，"好的。"

　　马赛曲和英国国歌打断了女王的谈话。不过，宾主就座之后，女王又和总统继续谈刚才的话题。

　　"他喜欢同性，还坐过牢，但他真有他自己说的那么坏吗？或者，更准确地说，"女王拿起了汤匙，"他有那么好吗？"

1　让·热内（Jean Genet, 1910—1986），法国著名且有争议的怪才作家，早年曾是流浪汉、小偷，作品于低俗中见奇异，自传体小说《小偷日记》毫不忌讳地描写饱尝耻辱的底层生涯。

事先并没有人告知总统，会谈的内容包括这个他一无所知的剧作家和小说家，他气恼地四处张望，寻找自己的文化部长，但她正忙着和坎特伯雷大主教交谈。

　　"你读过让·热内吧？"女王试探性地问道。

　　"当然。"总统回答。

　　"我对他挺感兴趣的。"女王说道。

　　"是吗？"总统说着放下了汤匙。这将是个漫长的夜晚。

· · ·

　　这都是那些狗惹的祸。女王的狗都是势利眼，通常在花园里遛过之后，就跑上前门的台阶，等着男仆给它们开门了。可是今天不知什么缘故，它们沿着平台疯跑狂叫，还从台阶跑下去，跑到王宫的另一边去。女王听见它们在那里冲着院子里的什么东西汪汪直叫。

　　在厨房门外的垃圾桶旁，停靠着一辆类似搬运车的卡车，原来那是威斯敏斯特城区的流动图书馆。女王对白金汉宫里的这一片不怎么熟悉，这个图书馆更是从没见过。显然她的狗也觉得新鲜，所以还在闹个不停。女王无法让它们安静下来，只好走上车，打算道个歉。

司机背朝她坐着，正在往书上贴标签。唯一的借书人是个瘦瘦的、姜黄色头发的男孩，他穿着白色工作服，正蜷坐在过道里看书。两个人都没注意到女王的出现，她只好咳嗽一声，然后说："这么喧扰，实在抱歉。"听到女王的声音，司机赶紧起身，结果一头撞在参考书的书架上，那个男孩跌跌撞撞地从地上站起来，碰翻了摄影与时尚类图书的书架。

女王将头伸出车外，冲着她的狗说："你们这些傻小子歇一会吧，别叫了。"这样一来，司机兼图书管理员总算有时间镇定下来，男孩也把地上的书都捡起来了。

"我以前从没在这儿见过你，你是……"

"我叫哈钦斯，陛下。每周三我都来。"

"是吗？我都不知道。你来的地方远吗？"

"不远，就在威斯敏斯特，陛下。"

"那你是……"

"我叫诺曼，陛下。诺曼·希金斯。"

"你在哪儿工作？"

"在厨房，陛下。"

"噢。你有很多时间读书吗？"

"其实没有，陛下。"

"我也一样。不过，我现在既然来了，不妨就借本书吧。"

哈钦斯先生的笑容里满是鼓励的神情。

"你有什么书可以推荐吗？"

"陛下喜欢哪一类的书呢？"

女王不禁有些犹豫，因为坦白地说，她自己也不清楚。她从来对读书就没有多大兴趣。当然，她也会读点书，但喜爱读书可不是她做的事。那是一种嗜好，而她的工作根本就不允许她有任何嗜好。无论是慢跑，种花，下棋，还是攀岩，装饰蛋糕，做航模，这些都不行。有嗜好就有偏爱，而她必须要避免偏爱，因为偏爱会排斥一些人。女王从不偏爱，她的工作是让别人感兴趣，而不是自己沉湎其中。此外，读书并非实干，而她一向是个实干家。所以女王来回打量着车上满满的书，尽量拖延着时间。"我可以借书吗？没有借书证也行？"

"没问题。"哈钦斯先生说。

"我算退休人士。"女王说。她知道这并不重要。

"您可以借六本书。"

"六本？这么多啊！"

这时那个姜黄色头发的年轻人已经选好了书给图书管理员盖章。为了再磨蹭一会时间，女王拿起了这本书。

"希金斯先生，你借了什么书？"她心里盘算着这会是一本什么样的书。虽然女王没有确切的想法，但她显然绝没想到会是这本。"噢，是塞西尔·比顿[1]。你认识他吗？"

"不认识，陛下。"

"那是自然。你太年轻了。他以前常待在这里，四处拍照。有点不好对付。一会儿站在这里，一会儿站在那里，啪啪地拍照。现在有本写他的书了？"

"有好几本了，陛下。"

"是吗？我想每个人迟早都会有人写的。"

女王很快地翻阅了一下。"书里也许有我的照片。对了，就是这张。当然，他不仅是摄影师，还是设计师。

---

[1] 塞西尔·比顿（Sir Cecil Beaton, 1904—1980），英国时尚、肖像和战争摄影师，同时还是记者、画家、室内设计师和获得奥斯卡金像奖的舞美服装设计师，曾与伊丽莎白二世合拍王室全家福。

他担任过《俄克拉荷马》之类的音乐剧的艺术设计。"

"我记得是《窈窕淑女》，陛下。"

"哦，是吗？"女王问道。她不习惯有人对她出言反驳。

"你刚才说你在哪儿工作？"她把书还给男孩。男孩的手又大又红。

"在厨房，陛下。"

女王还没有解决自己的问题。她知道，如果自己不借一本书就离开的话，哈钦斯先生会觉得这个图书馆的书不够齐备。这时，她在一架破旧的书里看到一个熟悉的名字。"艾维·康普顿-伯内特[1]！我可以借这本。"她取下这本书给哈钦斯先生盖章。

"真是太好了！"她装模作样地先将书拥在怀中，然后才打开它。"哦。这本书上一次借出是1989年。"

"她并不怎么受欢迎，陛下。"

"怎么会？我封了她做女爵士。"

1　艾维·康普顿-伯内特（Dame Ivy Compton-Burnett，1884—1969），作品主题集中在维多利亚后期上层阶级的生活。《男仆，女仆》（1947）通常被认为她最好的作品。

这可不一定就能赢得公众的心啊，哈钦斯先生忍住没说出来。

女王看到封底的照片，笑着说："我记得这个发型。头上裹着一圈好像馅饼皮的头发。"哈钦斯先生知道女王的微笑意味着她要离去。"再见。"

哈钦斯先生向她低头致意。这是图书馆里的人交代的应对女王的礼仪，没想到这一天还真的来了。女王向花园走去，她的狗又开始狂叫了。诺曼拿着他的那本塞西尔·比顿，绕过一位在垃圾桶旁休息抽烟的厨师，回厨房去了。

哈钦斯先生关上卡车后门，开车离去。他思忖着，一本艾维·康普顿-伯内特的小说要读不少时间。他自己从来没读完过她的书。他想，女王借这本书不过是个礼貌的姿态。这当然没错。不过，他还是十分感激女王的这一姿态，因为这对他不仅意味着礼貌。市议会一直威胁要削减图书馆的经费，有这样一位尊贵的借阅者（市议会喜欢称之为顾客）的光顾，自然对他有益。

"我们有个流动图书馆，"当晚女王对她的丈夫说，"每周三来。"

"太好了。妙事不断啊。"

"你还记得《俄克拉荷马》吗？"

"当然。我们订婚的时候看的。"想起来有点不可思议，那时他还是个金发的翩翩少年。

"是塞西尔·比顿担任的艺术设计吗？"女王问道。

"不知道。我从来不喜欢那个家伙。穿绿鞋子。"

"味道真好。"

"那是什么？"

"一本书。我借的。"

"我想，他已经不在了。"

"谁？"

"那个叫比顿的家伙。"

"是的。全都不在了。"

"那个剧还不错。"

说完他就郁闷地唱着"啊，早晨多美好"去睡觉了。女王打开书，读了起来。

•••

　　接下来的这个周三，女王本来打算让一位宫廷女侍去帮她还书的。但她的私人秘书凯文·斯卡查德爵士一直缠着她，让她不得不和他事无巨细地讨论每日活动的细节。终于，女王忍不住在讨论参观一座道路研究实验室的行程时，突然告诉凯文爵士今天是周三，她要去流动图书馆还书。凯文爵士来自新西兰，一心想做大事，对自己的工作有点过分的热心。女王这么一说，他也只得收拾起公文离开，心里却有点迷惑：女王的宫殿里就有好几个图书馆，她为什么还要去流动图书馆呢？

　　没有了狗的喧闹，女王这次来得比较安静。不过，流动图书馆里唯一的读者还是诺曼。

　　"您觉得这本书怎么样，陛下？"哈钦斯先生问。

　　"艾维女爵士？有点乏味。你注意到没有，书里每个人说话都一个腔调？"

　　"老实告诉您，她的书我从来都只读个开头。陛下读了多少？"

　　"都读完了。我一旦开始读一本书，就要把它读完。

我从小受的教育就是这样。书也好，面包、黄油和土豆泥也好，在我盘子里的就要吃完。我就是这样。"

"其实这本书您不必来还的。我们正在剔除一部分书。这个架子上的书想要都可以拿走。"

"你是说它就属于我了？"女王抱紧了书。"我还真是来对了。下午好，希金斯先生。你借的还是塞西尔·比顿？"

诺曼将他看的书递给女王，这是本关于大卫·霍克尼[1]的书。女王翻阅了一下，泰然自若地看着书里那些青年男子的臀部。他们或是在加州的游泳池中，或是躺在纷乱的床上。

"有些作品，"她说，"有些作品似乎还没有完成。这幅肯定是给弄脏了。"

"我觉得这就是他的风格，陛下，"诺曼说，"他其实画得很好。"

女王再次仔细打量着诺曼。"你真是在厨房工作？"

1　大卫·霍克尼（David Hockney，1937— ），英国画家、摄影师，当代最具影响力的英国艺术家之一。女王曾授予他限量 24 枚的"功绩勋章"。

"是的，陛下。"

女王其实并没有打算再借一本书，但她觉得，既然来了，不借书倒有点犯难。不过，要挑选哪本书呢？像上周一样，她又被难住了。事实上，女王根本就不想再读一本书，更不想再读一本艾维·康普顿-伯内特的书。读完艾维的书实在不容易。还好，她的运气不错，这次碰巧看到了一本再版的南希·米特福德[1]的《爱的追寻》。她拿起书，对哈钦斯先生说："就借这本吧。她的妹妹是不是嫁了那个姓莫斯利的[2]？"

哈钦斯先生回答说他记得是的。

"她另一个妹妹的婆母是我以前的服装侍从女官长[3]

1　南希·米特福德（Nancy Mitford，1904—1973），英国小说家、传记作家和记者，20世纪初社交界著名而富争议的"米特福德六姊妹"之一。她的小说描写英法上流社会的生活，以犀利和颇为挑衅的幽默文笔著称。

2　指奥斯瓦德·莫斯利（Sir Oswald Mosley，1896—1980），英国法西斯分子，创建英国法西斯联盟。1936年娶戴安娜·米特福德，阿道夫·希特勒曾作为荣誉嘉宾出席婚礼。

3　服装侍从女官长（Mistress of the Robes）为英国王室高级女官。黛博拉·米特福德的婆母、玛德文郡公爵夫人玛丽·卡文迪什1953至1967年曾任该职。

吧？"

"我不太清楚，陛下。"

"她还有个妹妹挺惨的，跟过希特勒。[1] 还有一个妹妹是共产党。[2] 我记得另外还有一个。不过写这本书的是南希？"

"是的，陛下。"

"很好。"

几乎没有一部小说像这样有人缘，女王原本的担心也都烟消云散了。她满怀信心地将书给哈钦斯先生盖章。

女王选择《爱的追寻》既十分幸运，又极为重要。如果她选的是另一本乏味的书，比如说一本乔治·艾略特的早期作品，或是一本亨利·詹姆斯的晚期作品，作为读书新手，她很可能会就此放弃读书。她可能会想，读书和工作没有区别。那我们也就没有故事可讲了。

女王很快就迷上了这本书。那天晚上，公爵拿着热水瓶，经过女王卧室的时候，听见她在朗声大笑。他把

---

1 指尤妮蒂·米特福德，希特勒的狂热追随者。
2 指杰西卡·米特福德，作家、记者、民权活动和政治活动家，1944年加入美国籍。

头靠在门上倾听片刻，对屋里说："嗨，你还好吧？"

"没事。我在读书。"

"又读？"他摇着头走了。

第二天早上，女王的鼻子有点不通。因为没有事先安排的工作，她索性留在床上，声称自己感冒了。这不是女王一贯的作风。其实，她这么做只是为了继续读那本书。

整个国家都知道"女王得了轻微的感冒"。然而，女王和大家都不知道的是，这只不过是她因为读书而做出的一系列变化的开始。其中不少变化都影响深远。

隔了一天，女王和她的私人秘书例行见面，讨论的事务之一就是今天通称的人力资源。

女王对她的秘书说："我们以前的名称是'人事'。"其实以前的名称是"仆人"。她也提到过"仆人"这个名称，但遭到了凯文爵士的反驳。

"那会被人曲解的，陛下，"凯文爵士说，"您不能让公众产生一丝反感。'仆人'这个名称会传递错误的讯息。"

女王说："至少对我来说，人力资源这个词没有任何意义。不过，既然我们讨论的是人力资源，现在我想提拔厨房里的一个人力资源。至少要把他调到楼上来。"

凯文爵士没有听过希金斯这个名字，问了几个下属才知道诺曼是谁。

"我实在不理解，"女王说，"他怎么会被分到厨房去。这个年轻人看上去很聪明。"

侍从告诉凯文爵士："诺曼长得不好看，有点瘦，姜黄色的头发。陛下怎么发慈悲了。"

凯文爵士说："陛下似乎挺喜欢他，想把他调到楼上来。"

诺曼就这样从整天洗盘子的生活中解放了出来。他穿上了还不太合身的侍从制服，成了一名宫廷侍从。可想而知，他首先要做的事肯定与图书馆有关。

接下来的周三女王要参加在纽尼顿举行的体操比赛，就让诺曼去帮她还书。女王交代他，南希·米特福德的这本书似乎还有续集，她也想看，此外，再借几本他觉得她会喜欢的书。

这项任务让诺曼有点焦虑不安。虽然他读的书不少，但他是自学成才的，选择书的标准主要是看作者是否喜欢同性。虽然这个范围还比较宽泛，但当他要帮别人挑选书的时候，就显得有所局限了。偏偏让他挑书的还是女王。

哈钦斯先生也帮不上忙。不过，他觉得写狗的作品也许女王会感兴趣，这倒让诺曼想起，自己读过的 J. R. 阿克利[1]的小说《我的小狗郁金香》可能合适。哈钦斯先生有点迟疑，提醒诺曼这是本同性恋小说。

"是吗？我都没意识到。她会认为就是关于狗的吧。"诺曼天真地说。

他带着借的书来到宫里女王的住所，碰巧遇到公爵。他记起要尽量少出现的训示，就赶紧躲在一座法国细木工橱柜后面。

公爵过后告诉女王："今天下午看见了奇景——姜色木棒当侍从。"

女王回答："那肯定是诺曼。我和他在流动图书馆里认识的。他以前在厨房工作。"

1　J. R. 阿克利（J. R. Ackerley，1896—1967），英国作家、编辑，出版了许多日后在英国具有影响力的新兴诗人和作家。他是公开的同性恋者，这在他的时代非常罕见。

公爵说："那倒适合他。"

女王说："他很聪明。"

公爵说："长成那样，不聪明就完了。"

过后女王对诺曼说："郁金香，给狗起这样的名字倒很有趣。"

诺曼说："这本书算是小说，只不过作者生活中真的有只狗，是只阿尔萨斯狗。所以这其实是部隐晦的自传，陛下。"

他没有告诉女王那只阿尔萨斯狗的名字叫奎尼。[1]

女王问："哦，为什么要这样隐晦呢？"

诺曼想，女王看了书就会明白的，不过他没这么说。

"他的朋友都不喜欢他的狗，陛下。"

女王说："我很理解他的感受。"诺曼严肃地点了点头。的确，王室的狗从来就不受欢迎。女王开心地笑了，这诺曼真是不错。她知道自己的威严会让他人感觉压抑、畏缩不前，几乎没有仆人敢在她面前显露出真性

---

1 奎尼（Queenie）既是女性的名字，也是女王伊丽莎白二世的昵称，还可以指喜欢同性的男子。

16

情。诺曼虽然有点古怪，但他从不掩饰自己，也不会装腔作势。这倒是很少见的。

不过，女王知道了真相可能会不高兴：诺曼之所以没被她的威严吓倒，是因为他觉得女王年纪太大了。她的年龄消解了王权的威严。她是女王，但同时也是位老太太。诺曼以前在泰恩莱德的养老院工作，所以他可不怕老太太。对他来说，女王是他的雇主，但她的年龄让她不仅是女王，更像他以前照顾的病人。不管怎么说，无论作为女王，还是作为病人，他都要迎合她。但是，没过多久，诺曼的这些想法就没了。他发现女王敏锐精明，自己白白浪费了许多精力。

女王是个非常传统的人。当她开始读书的时候，她觉得应该在合适的地方——宫里的图书馆——做这件事情。虽然有图书馆之名，里面也的确藏书满满，但却很少有人在这儿读书。人们在这里发出最后通牒，确定政策底线，编撰祈祷书或是决定婚姻大事，可如果想舒舒服服地坐着读书，宫里的图书馆绝不是个合适的地方。就算想要拿本书都不容易，比如在所谓的开架区域，所有的书都放在锁着的镀金格栏后面。不少书都价值连城，这就让人更不想去那里读书了。所以，读书最好别在专门读书的地方。女王觉得可能就是这么个道理，便又回到了楼上。

女王读完南希·米特福德的续集《爱在冰雪纷飞时》，欣喜地发现米特福德还写了其他不少书。尽管有些可能是历史题材的，但她还是将这些书都列入了自己新近开列的书单。然后她开始读诺曼选的书——J. R. 阿克利的小说《我的小狗郁金香》。她想自己是否见过他呢？应该没有。正如诺曼说的，女王喜欢这本书，因为书中的狗似乎比她的狗还多，而且同样不受欢迎。她发现阿克利写过一本自传，就让诺曼到伦敦图书馆去借。虽然女王是伦敦图书馆的资助者，但她从来没去过。当然，诺曼也没去过。他回来后特别兴奋，惊叹不已，对女王说那种图书馆他以前只在书上看到过，原以为现在已经不存在了。他在迷宫一样的书架中穿行，目眩神迷，感叹他（也许应该是她）居然有这么多的书可借。诺曼的热情十分具有感染力。女王想，下一次自己要和他一起去。

读完阿克利的自传后，女王发现，不出意料，他喜欢同性，还在 BBC 工作过。当然，对他的凄惨生活女王也颇为同情。阿克利的狗让她着迷，但她接受不了他对狗那种近乎兽医式的亲密。女王有点惊讶的是，看起来王宫卫兵似乎真像书中所写的那样有空接私活，而且要价合理。虽然她很想多了解一些，而且有些侍从以前当过卫兵，但还是不便打听这方面的情况。

书中写到了 E. M. 福斯特[1]。她记得在授予他荣誉勋爵的时候，曾见过他半小时。那次会见颇为尴尬。他畏畏缩缩的，有点像老鼠，几乎不说话，声音又小。女王觉得无法和他交流。尽管如此，他还是有点内秀的。当时他坐在那里，紧握两手，像是从《爱丽丝漫游奇境》里出来的人物，一点也看不出他在想什么。女王后来在他的传记里读到，福斯特说如果她是个男孩子，自己肯定会爱上她。这让她既惊讶，又开心。

女王意识到，福斯特自然是无法当面对她说这样的话的。不过，随着书读得越来越多，她越加遗憾自己居

1　E. M. 福斯特（E. M. Forster，1879—1970），英国著名作家，代表作有《印度之行》《看得见风景的房间》《霍华德庄园》等。

然如此让人畏惧。她尤其希望作家可以有勇气对她说出那些他们后来写下来的话。女王发现，书与书之间彼此相连，自己开始不断地接触新的领域，根本没有时间读完所有自己感兴趣的书。

女王还为自己错失了很多机缘而懊恼。她在孩童时代见过梅斯菲尔德[1]和沃尔特·德拉·梅尔[2]。当然，那时她和他们没什么可谈的，但她后来接见过 T. S. 艾略特、普利斯特列[3]、菲利普·拉金[4]和泰德·休斯[5]。女王挺喜欢休斯的，但他在她面前还是有点拘谨。因为那时她几乎没怎么看过这些作家的作品，所以她和他们无从谈起，

1　约翰·梅斯菲尔德（John Masefield，1878—1967），英国诗人、作家、剧作家，1930 年被任命为英国第 22 位"桂冠诗人"，直至 1967 年去世。
2　沃尔特·德拉·梅尔（Walter de la Mare，1873—1956），英国诗人、短篇小说作家和小说家，以其儿童文学作品最为著名。
3　J. B. 普利斯特列（J. B. Priestley，1894—1984），英国小说家、剧作家和广播节目主持人，笔下很多戏剧围绕着时间旅行的主题展开，代表作为《好伙伴》（1929）。
4　菲利普·拉金（Philip Larkin，1922—1985），英国现代诗人、小说家，被公认为继 T. S. 艾略特之后 20 世纪最有影响力的英国诗人。
5　泰德·休斯（Ted Hughes，1930—1988），英国诗人和儿童作家，被认为是他那个时代最杰出的诗人之一，从 1984 年起任英国"桂冠诗人"。休斯是美国自白派女诗人西尔维娅·普拉斯的丈夫。

交流甚少。他们说的话也没什么意思。真是浪费了大好机缘！

女王和凯文爵士说起这件事。这可真是找错了人。

"陛下当时肯定应该事先听过情况介绍吧？"

"当然了，"女王说，"但是情况介绍不能和读书相提并论。事实上，这两者是截然相反的。情况介绍要求简明，讲究的是事实和中肯。读书有点凌乱和散漫，总是让人心动。对同一个题目，情况介绍是封闭性的，而读书则是发散性的。"

凯文爵士说："陛下，我们是否还是继续讨论您参观鞋厂的行程呢？"

"下次再谈吧。"女王有点不耐烦地说。"我的书在哪儿呢？"

•••

女王发现了读书的妙处之后，一心想让别人也受益。

在去北安普顿的路上，她问司机："夏默斯，你平时阅读吗？"

"陛下，阅读什么？"

"你读书吗？"

"有机会的话我会读的，陛下。不过我好像一直都没时间。"

"许多人都这么说。我们要找出时间来读书。比如说今天早上，待会儿你要在市政厅外面等我。这时间就可以用来读书。"

"我要看着车子呢，陛下。这里是英格兰中部，到处都有人故意破坏东西。"

夏默斯将女王安全送抵之后，郡长将女王接入市政厅。他在车周围巡视了一圈，然后就在车里坐下来休息。阅读？他当然读了，人人都读的。他打开车里的小杂物箱，拿出《太阳报》[1]读起来。

有些人对阅读这个话题更感兴趣。特别是诺曼。女王对他从不隐瞒自己作为读者的不足，以及自己在文化艺术方面的欠缺。

一天下午，当他们两人在图书馆里阅读的时候，女

---

1 英国发行量最大的报纸，政治立场偏重中下阶层保守派民众。《太阳报》曾多次把国家元首、大事拿来开玩笑。有批评指其内容低俗、煽情，新闻手法不专业，惯以哗众取宠刺激销量。

王对诺曼说："你知道我真正擅长的是哪个方面吗？"

"不知道，陛下。"

"智力问答。我去过世界各地，见多识广。如果问起津巴布韦的首都，或是新南威尔士州的主要出口商品，那真是易如反掌。不过流行音乐和有些体育项目的题目可能有点难。"

"我可以负责流行音乐方面的题目。"诺曼说。

女王说："对啊，我们两人组一个队肯定厉害。嗯，未走过的路，谁说的？"

"谁啊，陛下？"

"未走过的路。查一下。"

诺曼查了《名言辞典》，找到了答案：作者是罗伯特·弗罗斯特[1]。

"我想到一个说你的词。"女王说。

"说我的？"

"你听我差遣，为我去图书馆借书、查字典找偏僻

---

1 罗伯特·弗罗斯特（Robert Frost，1874—1963），美国著名诗人，曾四度获得普利策奖。上文指的是弗罗斯特诗篇《未走过的路》（"The Road Not Taken"）。

字、查找名言。你知道这叫什么吗？"

"我以前是干粗活的仆人，陛下。"

"你现在可不是这样了。你是我的文书。"

诺曼查了女王放在办公桌上的字典，文书的意思是"笔录口授，抄写手稿的人，相当于文学助理"。

这位新的文书在走廊上靠近女王办公室的地方有张椅子。当他不用待命或为女王办事的时候，就可以坐在椅子上读书。这让其他的侍从对诺曼很有意见，觉得他实在太舒服了，而且他根本没有好到可以这样享受的份上。时不时地有经过的侍从会停下来问诺曼，他是不是除了读书没有别的事情可做。一开始诺曼被问住了，答不上来。后来被问多了，他就回答说他是在为女王陛下读书。虽然这通常也是实话，但听起来总是让人不舒服，这些问话的侍从只得恨恨地离开。

•••

随着读的书越来越多，女王开始从各个图书馆，包括她自己的图书馆里借书。不过，出于对流动图书馆和哈钦斯先生的感情，她有时还是会去停在厨房院子里的流动图书馆借书。

然而，一个星期三的下午，流通图书馆没有来，接下来的一周它也没来。诺曼去找人询问，结果被告知，流动图书馆不来宫里是因为政府全面的经费缩减。他没有就此罢休，一直追到皮姆利科的一个学校，发现哈钦斯先生在那里工作，还是坐在车里往书上贴着标签。哈钦斯先生告诉他，尽管他向图书馆的外联部指出女王是他们的读者之一，但图书馆的理事会根本不予理会。理事会说他们在做出这一决定之前征询过宫里的意见，宫里表示对此事毫无兴趣。

诺曼气愤地把这一切告诉女王，她似乎倒不为所动。不过，虽然她对诺曼没说什么，但这件事证实了她的猜测：在王室中，读书本身，或者说女王对读书的喜爱没有得到认可。

失去流动图书馆不过是个小挫折。这件事至少有一个好结果：哈钦斯先生上了受勋名单。诚然，他获得的勋奖并不高，但和他同时受勋的都是对女王有特殊贡献，或为女王个人效过力的。这件事也没有得到认可。凯文爵士尤其反对。

凯文·斯卡查德爵士来自新西兰，对他的任命似乎意味着王室的某种变化，所以当时媒体是一片欢呼，认为这个（还算）年轻的人将像一把新扫帚那样，将君主制里长年累积下来的过度的顺从和令人反感的恭维一扫而空。按照这个说法，王室犹如郝维辛小姐的婚宴——结满蜘蛛网的水晶吊灯，爬满老鼠的婚礼蛋糕，而凯文爵士就会像皮普那样撕开朽烂的窗帘，让阳光照进屋里。[1]女王以前也曾充满活力，所以这种假想难以让她信服。她反而觉得这股清新的澳洲来风最终会把它自己给吹走的。私人秘书和首相一样，来来往往，不断更换。女王觉得，对凯文爵士来说，她可能不过是块踏脚石。他毕业于哈佛商学院，必定是要在商界找一份高层工作的。凯文爵士公开宣布的工作目标之一就是让王室更接近大众。按照他的话来说，就是"展示我们的马厩"。开放白金汉宫，偶尔在王宫花园里举办音乐会、演唱会和其他活动，都是在往这个方向努力。但是，女王对读

---

1 狄更斯小说《远大前程》中，孤儿皮普被雇为怪异的老处女郝维辛小姐的陪侍。郝维辛在结婚当天被新郎抛弃，此后家中一直保留着婚宴的布置，几十年后房间里蛛网密布，覆满霉菌，一切都已经腐烂。

书的执着让凯文爵士心神不宁。

"陛下，我认为读书虽然不是一种精英活动，但还是会让人误解。这会让一些人觉得被排斥在外的。"

"排斥在外？绝大多数人都能阅读吧？"

"陛下，他们是能读，但我觉得他们不一定会读。"

"凯文爵士，这样的话，我正好给他们树立了一个好榜样。"

女王温和地笑着说。她注意到，和刚任命时相比，近来凯文爵士的新西兰气质少多了。现在他的口音只有一点点新西兰腔。女王知道他对此很敏感，不喜欢有人提起。这是诺曼告诉他的。

另一个微妙的问题是他的名字。凯文爵士认为自己的名字是个负担：如果让他本人来选，他绝不会选凯文这个名字。他不喜欢自己的名字，所以他对女王叫他名字的次数分外敏感。每次女王叫他名字的时候，他都感到十分屈辱。这一点他觉得女王是不会了解的。

事实上，女王对此心知肚明，这当然又是诺曼告诉她的。不过，对她而言，人的名字，穿的衣服，声音和出身等等，这所有的一切都不重要。她是一位真正的民主主义者。也许是这个国家里仅有的一位。

但在凯文爵士看来，女王实在没有必要这么频繁地叫他的名字。而且，他十分肯定，女王有时在叫他名字的时候带上了一点新西兰腔，让人不禁联想起那里遍地的羊群和慵懒的周日下午。作为英联邦的元首，女王曾数次访问过新西兰，公开表示过十分喜爱那个国家。

凯文爵士说："陛下应该保持精力集中，这非常重要。"

"凯文爵士，你说的'精力集中'是指我应该只关注中心吧。我已经这样过了五十多年，现在可以时不时地看看边缘了。"女王觉得自己的暗示可能有点过了，还好凯文爵士没注意到。

他回答说："我可以理解。陛下需要消磨时间。"

"消磨时间？"女王说。"读书可不是在消磨时间，而是在了解他人的生活和大千世界。这和消磨时间根本风马牛不相及。我只希望自己能多读点书。凯文爵士，如果我想消磨时间的话，我就去新西兰了。"

女王连叫了两次他的名字，提了一次新西兰，凯文爵士只得伤心地告退。不过，他说的话倒也并非全无道理。凯文爵士走了之后，女王十分困扰，反复思考着自己为何会此时突然对读书感兴趣。她究竟从哪里来的动力呢？

毕竟，很少有人像她这样见多识广。她几乎去过所有的国家，见过所有的名人。女王本人正是这大千世界的重要部分。现在她怎么会被书迷住了呢？不管怎么说，书只不过是反映世界、描述世界的啊！读书？她可是真正见过世面的！

"我认为我喜欢读书是因为我有责任了解人性。"女王对诺曼这样说。这个说法太陈腐了，诺曼根本就没听进去。他觉得自己可没有这样的责任，读书纯粹是为了乐趣，而不是为了获得启迪。当然了，他也知道，部分的乐趣正来自读书中获得的启迪。但责任和读书的乐趣毫无关系。

从女王的身份背景来说，责任从来都是优先于乐趣的。如果她觉得自己有责任读书，那她就可以堂堂正正地读。即使阅读的过程中有乐趣，那也是偶然的。可是，现在她为何会沉湎于读书的乐趣呢？女王没有和诺曼讨论这个问题。她觉得这源自她的秉性和地位。

女王认为，读书的魅力在于书籍的漠然：文学都有一种高傲的味道，根本不在乎它们的读者是谁，也不在乎有没有读者。包括她自己在内，所有的读者都是平等的。文学就是一个联邦，而字母就是一个共和国。女王确实在毕业典礼、荣誉学位授予典礼等场合听到过字母共和国这种说法，但她以前并不知道它的含义。那时，提到任何的共和国字眼，她都会认为是对她的无礼。当她的面用这个词再怎么说都显得有点不得体。直到现在她才明白这个词的真正含义。书籍不会唯命是从。所有的读者都一样。这让女王回想起自己年轻的时候。那时她最兴奋的一次经历就是在欧洲胜利日的当晚，她和妹妹溜出王宫，混入了欢庆的人群，结果没有人认出她们。她觉得，阅读与那次的经历有点像，全都不问姓名，可以与他人分享，又普通寻常。女王过了一辈子与众不同的生活，现在她渴望这种普通的生活。在每一本书里，她都可以找到这样的感觉。

这些疑问和自省不过是起点。一旦女王开始充满信心地读书，她就会觉得想读书并不奇怪，而那些一度让她小心翼翼的书籍，也渐渐成为她生活的一部分。

......

　　女王承担的王室职责之一是每年宣布国会开启。之前她并没有觉得这项工作是个负担，反而挺喜爱它的。尽管同样的仪式已经举行了五十年，但对她来说，在秋高气爽的早晨，坐车经过圣詹姆斯公园里的林荫大道依然是种享受。可是，现在她不这样想了。一想到整个仪式要进行两个小时，女王就很头痛。好在车厢不是敞开式的，她可以带着书坐在车里。她很擅长一边看书一边向外挥手，其中的秘诀就是把书放在车窗以下的位置，注意力集中在书上，不去管车外的人群。公爵对此十分不以为然，但对女王来说这样比不看书好多了。

　　出发前一切进行得都很顺利。直到她坐进车里，拿起眼镜的时候，女王才意识到自己忘了带书，而车队已经在王宫前院里整装待发了。她不管车里公爵的怒气和车外马车夫的烦躁，在马匹的骚动声和马具的叮当声中给诺曼打了电话。王宫卫兵全部稍息，整队人马都在等候。仪式的负责人看了看手表，发现已经晚了两分钟。他知道女王最不喜欢迟到，而且他对书的事也一无所知。

不过，没有女王的命令他也不敢轻举妄动。就在此时，诺曼穿过前院的砂石路轻快地跑了过来，小心地将藏在披肩下的书送给了女王。这样大队人马才出发离开王宫。

坐在车上的女王夫妇并不愉快。两人各自往窗外挥手，公爵挥得特别用力，而女王则有点无精打采。车走得也有点快，以便赶上刚才迟的两分钟。

车到威斯敏斯特的时候，女王悄悄地将这本引起不快的书放在一个靠垫后面，准备回程的时候接着看。然后她小心地登上御座，开始发表讲话。女王觉得这个指定自己向全国民众发表的讲话真是无趣之极，总是"我的政府将会这样做……我的政府将会那样做"这类的话。讲话既没有文采，也缺乏格调和趣味。女王觉得这个讲话根本不堪卒读。这一次，由于她要补上迟到的两分钟，所以读得更有些杂乱无章。

回到车上后，女王总算松了一口气。她伸手去拿自己放在靠垫后面的书，却发现书没了。随着马车隆隆地前进，女王一面依然向窗外挥着手，一面暗自在其他靠垫后面摸索。

"不是你坐在上面吧？"

"坐在什么上面？"

"我的书。"

"我没有。这里有些皇家军团的人，有些还坐着轮椅。赶紧挥手吧！"

回到王宫之后，女王找来了当天负责的侍从，年轻的格兰特。他告诉女王，当她在上议院讲话的时候，警犬来过，那本书被特工没收了。他估计那本书可能被炸掉了。

"炸掉了？"女王反问道。"那可是本安妮塔·布鲁克纳[1]的小说。"

这位年轻的侍从似乎对女王一点也不恭敬。他说特工认为那可能是个危险装置。

女王说："这倒对了。那就是个装置。书就是点燃你想象力的装置。"

侍从格兰特回答："是的，陛下。"

---

[1] 安妮塔·布鲁克纳（Anita Brookner，1928— ），布克奖获奖小说家、艺术史学家，1990 年受封二等勋位爵士。布鲁克纳被誉为英语的文体家，小说人物多为欧陆移民后代，作品探讨情感的缺失和融入社会的困难，尤其是中产阶级知识妇女遭受的情感孤立。

他听上去像在和他的祖母说话。女王意识到，这不过是泼向自己读书热情的又一盆冷水。这让她有些不快。

她对格兰特说："很好。那你就去告诉特工，让他们负责找一本同样的书，检查过没有炸弹后，明早放在我桌上。还有一件事。马车上的靠垫太脏了。看把我的手套弄的。"然后扬长而去。

"他妈的。"侍从骂骂咧咧地从自己的马裤里拿出了那本书。这是上头让他藏的。不过令人意外的是，官方没有发表任何关于仪式延迟的说明。

女王的狗也不喜欢她的这个新嗜好。以前她遛狗的时候，总是放纵它们在院子里喧闹嬉戏，现在只要一走出王宫，女王马上就在最近的椅子上坐下来看书。她不再和它们玩掷球和拣棍的游戏，也不会对它们故作嗔怒，最多不时扔给它们一块吃剩的饼干，这让它们的每次出游都很无趣。这些狗被惯坏了，脾气很大，但毕竟没有那么笨，所以没过多久它们就开始痛恨书，认为书总在扫它们的兴。

一旦女王有书掉在地上，她身边的狗就会立刻跳上去，口涎横流地将书咬着跑到王宫的另一头，然后心满意足地将书撕得粉碎。虽然得过詹姆斯·泰特·布莱克奖[1]，伊恩·麦克尤恩的书，甚至 A. S. 拜厄特的书都难逃此劫。女王虽然是伦敦图书馆的资助人，但因为这样不断丢书，还是得反复给图书馆的续借管理员打电话道歉。

女王的狗还讨厌诺曼。凯文爵士也不喜欢他。他觉得女王对文学的热情至少有一部分是诺曼的责任。此外，每次凯文爵士和女王见面的时候，诺曼虽然不在旁边，但总是就在附近待命，经常在他们谈话时出现。凯文爵士对此很是气恼。

这一次他是在和女王商量两周后去威尔士的访问。他们讨论的具体行程包括乘坐巨型缆车，出席尤克里里琴音乐会，参观奶酪厂等，就在这时，女王起身走到门口。

"诺曼。"

凯文爵士听到诺曼站起来时椅子发出的摩擦声。

"过几周我们要去威尔士。"

"真糟糕，陛下。"

1　詹姆斯·泰特·布莱克奖（James Tait Black Memorial Prize）授予用英语写作的文学作品，与霍桑登奖同为英国最古老的文学奖项。

女王冲着面无表情的凯文爵士笑着说："诺曼就是这么没礼貌。我们已经读了迪伦·托马斯[1]，对吧？还有约翰·考柏·波伊斯[2]和简·莫里斯[3]。还有谁是威尔士的？"

诺曼说："您可以读基尔弗特[4]，陛下。"

"他是谁？"

"他是十九世纪的一个牧师，陛下。他住在威尔士边境，写了本日记。他喜欢小姑娘。"

女王说："哦，像刘易斯·卡罗尔？"[5]

"比他更糟，陛下。"

"啊。你能帮我借到他的日记吗？"

1　迪伦·托马斯（Dylan Thomas，1914—1953），20世纪最重要的威尔士诗人之一，在文体和意象上极有独创性，革新了英国现代诗歌。

2　约翰·考柏·波伊斯（John Cowper Powys，1872—1963），小说家、评论家和诗人，被视为托马斯·哈代文学上的继承者。

3　简·莫里斯（Jan Morris，1926—　），历史学家、游记作家，尤以大英帝国史《英国式和平》（Pax Britannica）三部曲著称。

4　弗朗西斯·基尔弗特（Francis Kilvert，1840—1879），英国牧师，著有多卷日记，描绘19世纪70年代英国乡村生活，在他死后五十多年发表，甫一出版即获评论界赞誉。日记坦陈了对年轻女孩的迷恋，有关于小女孩的大量描写，包括体罚的细节。

5　据称刘易斯·卡罗尔有和未成年女孩独处的怪癖，喜欢拍摄她们的裸体，这在现代人看来皆为"禁忌"。

"我会在书单上加上它的，陛下。"

女王关上门，回到办公桌前。

"你看，凯文爵士，我可是做了准备的。"

凯文爵士从没听说过基尔弗特，因此不为所动。

"这家奶酪厂在一个新的商业区。那里原来是一处废弃的煤矿。奶酪厂带动了整个区域的经济发展。"

"噢，没错，"女王说，"不过你得承认，文学也很重要。"

"我不知道。"凯文爵士回答。"下一个工厂是做电脑配件的。陛下将会为他们的餐厅剪彩。"

"我想会安排些歌唱节目吧？"女王问。

"会安排一个合唱团的，陛下。"

"一般都是这样。"

女王觉得凯文爵士的脸肌肉感很强，似乎双颊上也有肌肉。他一皱眉，双颊上就满是皱纹。她想，如果自己是个小说家的话，这倒是值得一写的。

"陛下，我们要保证合唱时大家手里都拿着同样的圣歌书。"

"在威尔士？当然了。肯定的。你家里最近怎么样？

在忙着剪羊毛吧？"

"剪羊毛不是在这个季节，陛下。"

"噢，还在放羊呢。"

女王深深一笑，表明会面已经结束。等她的私人秘书走到门口，向她鞠躬致意的时候，她已经又开始看书了。她头也没抬，只低声说了句"凯文爵士"就将书翻到了下一页。

•••

女王按时访问了威尔士、苏格兰、兰开夏郡和西南部，这样不间断的全国巡游是君主制的象征。女王需要见见她的臣民。不过这样的会面往往让这些臣民手足无措，张口结舌，这时候就需要侍从的帮忙了。

为了避免与女王见面时出现无话可说的情况，侍从们时常会给等待女王接见的人一些与女王谈话的提示。

"陛下可能会问你住得远不远。回答好这个问题就接着说你是坐火车还是自己开车来的。然后她可能会问你车停在哪里，这里的交通是不是比——你说你是从哪里来的？——安德沃要拥挤？女王对国家生活的各个方面都感兴趣，所以她有时候会谈谈如今在伦敦停车有多难。你就可以接着谈谈你在巴辛斯托克遇到的停车难问题。"

"我是在安德沃。不过在巴辛斯托克停车也很难。"

"你说的对。你知道怎么回事了吧？就是聊聊天。"

这样的对话虽然平庸，但它们的好处是容易把握，而且简短，这样女王就可以尽量缩短会面的时间。会面顺利又准时，女王高兴，接见的人也高兴。即使他们盼望一生的对话只不过是谈论 M6 公路上关闭的车道，也并不会失望。[1] 重要的是他们见到了女王，和她谈了话，然后大家都准时离开。

这样的会面不过是例行公事，所以侍从一般很少在旁提点，几乎都是远远地站着，脸上带着鼓励又有点傲慢的微笑。但是，他们发现最近女王接见的人里说不出话的越来越多，而且很多人与女王交谈的时候都不知所云。于是他们开始偷听，想知道女王究竟在说些什么。

侍从们逐渐得知，女王没有通知他们就改变了长期以来的会面辞令。她不再问接见的人工作时间的长短、

1　M6 是英国最长的一条公路，同时也是最繁忙的公路。

住得多远、家乡哪里这样的问题，而是一见面就问："你在读什么书？"几乎没人能答上这个问题，只有一个人说了句："圣经算吗？"由此而来的是对话的尴尬停顿。这时女王会说："我在读……"有时候她甚至还从自己的手提包里拿出那本书，给对方看一眼。意料之中的，接见变得既冗长又糟糕。不少喜爱女王的人离开时都懊悔自己表现得不好，觉得似乎吃了女王一记闷棍。

下班后，皮尔斯、特里斯特拉姆、贾尔斯、埃尔斯佩思这四位对女王忠心耿耿的仆人在一起讨论："你在读什么书？这算什么问题啊？哎哟，大多数人根本就不读书的。他们一这么说，陛下就立刻从手提包里拿出自己刚读完的书送给他们。"

"然后这些人转身就把书在 eBay 上卖掉。"

"一点不错。你们最近有没有跟随女王出巡过？"一位宫廷女侍插嘴说。"这件事已经传开了。以前人们觐见女王的时候会带点怪异的水仙花或是一束陈旧的樱草花，那时女王都是交给我们拿到后面去的。现在他们都是带着他们读的书来。还有人带他们写的书来。要是你不幸轮到在女王身边服侍的话，你肯定要个小推车才能拿得过来。我要是想找个推书车的工作，那我还不如去哈查德书店呢。我觉得陛下快变成那种难伺候的人了。"

侍从们心里不满，但还是尽量容忍。只不过他们以往的例行公事，不得不因为女王的新喜好而改变。在接见前的准备中，侍从们会暗示觐见者，女王陛下还是会像以前一样问他们来处可远，乘何种交通工具而来，但现在她很可能会问他们正在读什么书。

闻言至此，大多数人都摸不着头脑，有时还会惊慌失措。不过他们用不着沮丧：侍从们会给他们一堆建议的。这样做意味着女王会得到一些错误的印象：不仅安迪·麦克纳布[1]的读者远远超过实际情况，而且几乎所有的人都一致地喜爱乔安娜·特罗洛普[2]。可这并不重要。至少接见的过程不再有尴尬。而且，一旦觐见者准备好了答案，接见的过程就又变得顺利起来，可以像以前那样按时结束。唯一的问题是偶尔一两个觐见者会向女王表示自己喜爱弗吉尼亚·伍尔芙或是狄更斯，这就会引

1　安迪·麦克纳布（Andy McNab，1959— ），畅销惊悚小说家，曾为英国空军特别部队军士。

2　乔安娜·特罗洛普（Joanna Trollope，1943— ），英国言情小说家。

发一场热烈而漫长的讨论。也有不少希望能在女王这里找到知音的人说自己在读哈里·波特。女王没有时间读奇幻小说，所以她总是轻快地说："很好。这书我打算留着以后读。"然后就立刻进入下一个话题。

凯文爵士每天都要和女王见面。他总是对女王痴迷的读书唠叨不休，还提出了些新想法。"陛下，我们是否可以让您的阅读多元化一点。"以前女王可能听过就算了，但书读得越多她对术语的耐心就越差。更何况她一向就不喜欢术语。

"多元化？是什么意思？"

"我只是刚刚想到这件事，陛下。如果我们发布新闻公告，说明陛下不仅读英国文学，而且也读少数族裔文学，效果应该挺好的。"

"凯文爵士，你说的少数族裔文学是什么呢？《爱经》[1]吗？"

凯文爵士叹了口气。

---

1 《爱经》(The Kama Sutra)，古印度一本关于性爱、哲学和心理学的典籍。

"我在读维克拉姆·塞特[1]。他算吗？"

凯文爵士从没听说过这个作家，但他觉得这名字听起来像是个少数族裔作家。

"萨尔曼·拉什迪[2]呢？"

"他可能不算，陛下。"

女王说："我不明白，为什么我们要发个新闻公告呢？公众为什么要关心我读的书呢？他们知道女王在读书就够了。我想一般人都会说：'那又怎么样？'"

凯文爵士说："读书意味着逃避，意味着您没有空做其他的事。如果这个追求本身少一点……自私的味道，大家会更容易接受。"

"自私？"

"可能用自我中心更准确。"

"你说得有点过分了。"

凯文爵士不依不饶："要是我们能给您的阅读找个

1　维克拉姆·塞特（Vikram Seth，1952—　），印度小说家、诗人。

2　萨尔曼·拉什迪（Salman Rushdie，1947—　），出身印度穆斯林家庭，在英国长大，后定居纽约。小说代表作有《午夜的孩子》《摩尔人最后的叹息》等，1989年出版《撒旦诗篇》引起轩然大波，伊朗宗教领袖霍梅尼曾公开谴责此书并悬赏处死他。

冠冕堂皇的理由，比如和全国的文化教养联系起来，说是为了提高青年人的阅读水平……"

"我读书是为了乐趣，"女王说道，"这不是我的公众职责。"

凯文爵士说："也许它应该算是吧。"

晚上女王告诉公爵这件事的时候，他说："他真是太没礼貌了。"

•••

除了公爵，其他的王室成员怎么看女王的新爱好呢？女王对读书的热情对他们有什么影响呢？

如果女王负责的是做饭、购物和打扫清洁各处行宫（当然，这有点不可思议），那负面影响肯定十分明显。不过女王自然不用做这些事情。可能她去王室包厢看戏的次数少了，不过这并不影响她的丈夫和子女。女王的读书热情真正影响，或者用凯文爵士的话来说，"冲击"的是社会公众。人们开始看出来她在履行义务时有点勉强：她在参加奠基仪式的时候没有热情，为船只下水剪彩的时候也草草了事。总是有读不完的书在等着她。

这些事情可能会让女王的工作人员忧心忡忡，但她的家人反而有种解脱感。女王总是对他们严格要求，即使年岁渐长也没有一点放松。读书改变了女王。她变得宽容了，不再管制家人，他们总算可以生活得自由自在了，心里大呼读书万岁。不过，有时候日子也不好过。他们会被逼着读书，要和女王讨论读书的话题，还会被盘问自己的读书习惯。最可怕的是，有时女王会把一些书塞到他们手上，然后不久就来查问他们是否读了。

实际上，他们经常会在王宫里一些意想不到的地方见到她。女王总是鼻子上架着副眼镜在读书，身旁放着铅笔和笔记本。她通常会匆匆地抬头看他们一眼，然后略微举下手示意，敷衍了事。"嘿，你开心就好。"公爵会这样说着慢步走开。这倒是事实：女王的确十分快乐。她的热情无与伦比，读书的速度惊人。不过除了诺曼，也没人知道她读书的量如此惊人。

一开始，女王并不谈论自己的读书热情。在公开场合更是如此。她十分清楚，好比她忽然爱上了宗教或是大丽花，这种迟来的热情会让人觉得她有点奇怪。别人会想，她都这么大年纪了，干吗还自找麻烦呢？但对女王来说，现在没有比读书更重要的事情。就像有些作家无法停止写作，她也无法停止读书。到了这个年纪，有的人是注定要写作的，而她则是注定来读书的。

在刚开始读书的时候，女王有点诚惶诚恐，紧张不安。书的无穷无尽让她穷于应付，不知道如何前进。她读书没有体系，就是一本一本不断地读，有时候还同时读两三本书。过了一段时间，她开始记笔记了。她在阅读时总是手里拿着支铅笔，不是要写读书笔记，仅仅是摘录她觉得好的段落。这样过了一年之后，女王才尝试偶尔写下自己的感想。

"我觉得文学就像是一个广袤的国家，我在向它那遥远的边境前进，却无法到达。我启程太晚，永远也赶不上。"她这样写道。接下去的话有点风马牛不相及："繁文缛节可能令人不快，但窘迫尴尬更糟。"

在阅读过程中，女王也有些伤感。她第一次觉得自己错过了许多事情。在读西尔维亚·普拉斯[1]的传记时，

1　西尔维亚·普拉斯（Sylvia Plath，1932—1963），美国诗人、作家，成年后大部分时间里遭受抑郁症折磨，1963年自杀，此后争议继续围绕着她的生死、写作和文学遗产。

她感到不像这位女诗人那样坎坷真是幸运。不过，在读劳伦·白考尔[1]的回忆录时，她禁不住感叹白考尔小姐的人生要比她自己的精彩得多。她甚至有点嫉妒白考尔。这是女王以前没想到的。

从演员的自传到诗人自杀前的临终日志，女王这样读书似乎没有条理，也缺乏见识。但是，在刚开始的一段日子里，她觉得所有的书都是一样的。如同对待她的臣民那样，她觉得自己有责任不带成见地接近它们。对她而言，不存在具有教育意义的书，书就是一片未知的领域。她开始根本没有对它们加以区别。随着时间推移，女王逐渐有了自己的判断。但是，除了偶尔从诺曼那里听到只言片语，并没有人告诉她什么要读，什么不要读。劳伦·白考尔、威妮弗蕾德·霍尔特比[2]和西尔维亚·普拉斯——她们是谁呢？只有读过她才知道。

几周之后，女王在阅读的时候忽然抬起头问诺曼：

1　劳伦·白考尔（Lauren Bacall, 1924—2014），好莱坞黄金时代著名女演员，曾获奥斯卡终身成就奖。

2　威妮弗蕾德·霍尔特比（Winifred Holtby, 1898—1935），英国小说家、记者，代表作为长篇小说《南瑞丁》。

"你还记得我说过你是我的文书吗？我现在知道该如何称呼我自己了。我是个迟学者。"

诺曼查了手边的字典，读了出来："迟学者：晚年才开始学习的人。"

正是这种要弥补失去时间的心态，让女王以飞快的速度读着书。渐渐地，笔记中对书的评论增加了，同时她也更加自信了。和她处理生活中其他事情的风格一样，这些文学评论十分直率。女王不是位温和的读者。她时常希望书的作者就在身边，可以对他们训斥一番。

"不是只有我一个人想好好训一顿亨利·詹姆斯吧？"她这样写道。

"我能理解人们为何崇敬约翰逊博士[1]。不过，他的作品大多都是自以为是的废话吧？"

这一天的下午茶时间，女王正在读着亨利·詹姆斯。她高声喝道："嘿，快一点。"

女仆正推着餐车离开，赶紧说了句："对不起，陛

1　塞缪尔·约翰逊（Samuel Johnson，1709—1784），常称为约翰逊博士，英国影响极大的作家、文学批评家和词典编纂家。

下。"就在两秒钟内离开了房间。

"爱丽斯，我不是说你。"女王冲着她的背影说。她甚至追到门口说："我说的不是你。"

从前女王不会这样留心女仆，也不会在意自己伤了她的心。现在她却变了。坐回到椅子上之后，她不禁琢磨着原因何在。此时，女王还没有意识到，这种体谅正来自她读的书，包括那总是让人烦扰的亨利·詹姆斯。

虽然女王始终对自己失去了读书的大好时光耿耿于怀，但一想到她本可以和很多著名作家见面，但却放弃了机会，更让她遗憾不已。不过，对女王来说，这一点倒不难改变。在诺曼的催促下，她决定召见一些自己和诺曼都读过的作者。她觉得这样的会面肯定很有意思，说不定还充满乐趣。于是女王就安排了一个招待酒会（诺曼坚持称之为晚会）。

宫廷侍从原本以为，招待会的形式和以往王宫的花园宴会以及其他的大型招待酒会一样，需要事先通知那些女王可能想与其交谈的客人。可是女王觉得，这次的酒会采取这种形式不太合适，毕竟邀请的都是艺术家，所以她决定就自己随意走走。事实证明这不是个好主意。

这些作家通常在和女王单独见面的时候都表现得畏缩羞怯，但这会儿他们聚在一起就变得声音喧哗，谈论八卦。他们在大笑不已，可女王没觉得有什么特别可乐的。她总是徘徊在各个圈子外面，没人殷勤地招呼她。她感觉自己反倒成了客人。而她一旦开口，作家们的谈话往往戛然而止，大家都陷入难堪的沉默，还有些作家可能为了显示自己思想独立、经验老到，根本就不理会女王，自顾自地说下去。

女王曾经想过，和这些作家在一起会多么激动人心。她一直都渴望了解他们，甚至将他们当成自己的朋友。现在这些作家就在她面前，她阅读过他们的作品，且十分喜爱，然而，尽管她希望对他们表达仰慕之情，却一个字也说不出来。女王一生几乎从未害怕过，此时她却有点张口结舌，不知所措。只要说一句"我非常喜欢你的作品"就可以了，但是，过去这五十年来的镇静沉着和小心谨慎让她说不出口。为了有话可说，女王不得不掏出一些压箱底的东西来。不过不是"你住得离这儿有多远"，而是改成了与文学相关的问题。但是换汤不换药，还是一些老生常谈："你怎么看你作品中的人物？

你的工作时间有规律吗？你用文字处理软件吗？"女王知道问这些有点尴尬，但总比难堪的沉默好。

有个苏格兰作家特别让人害怕。女王问他的灵感从哪里来，他凶狠地说："灵感不是自己来的，陛下。要你去抓住它。"

女王后来结结巴巴地对一个作家表达了仰慕之情，希望他谈谈自己的创作经历，但她的热情却没有得到回应。在这种礼节上，男人实在比不上女人。这位作家对他写过的畅销书避而不说，而是大谈自己正在写的书。他一边喝着香槟，一边抱怨自己进展缓慢，所以是这个世界上最痛苦的人。

女王很快就得出结论，作家和他们笔下的人物一样都是读者想象的产物，因此最好还是读他们的书，而不是和他们见面。似乎这些作家从未意识到，别人读他们的书是帮了他们的忙。他们反而觉得自己写书是在给别人帮忙。

她一度打算定期举行这样的作家聚会，不过这天的这个晚会打消了她的念头。一次就足够了。凯文爵士一直对这事不热心。他对女王说，如果陛下为作家们举行了这样的酒会，就得再为艺术家们举行一次，紧跟而来还有科学家们。"陛下不能有所偏私。"现在可好，不会有这样的问题了。他总算松了口气。

凯文爵士认为这个文学色彩暗淡的晚会都是诺曼的错。这么说也有几分道理。因为当初女王才有这个想法的时候，就是诺曼一直在怂恿她。不过诺曼自己也不好过。因为请的是文学圈子的人，所以宾客中喜欢同性的大有人在。有些还是诺曼特地让女王请来的。但这没给他带来任何好处。和其他侍者一样，他也在负责端送酒和点心，而与其他侍者不同的是，他知道这些人的声望和地位。他甚至还读过他们的作品。可是，这些人并没有聚集在诺曼的周围，而是围着那些英俊的侍者和高大的宫廷侍从。诺曼后来伤心地抱怨说，这些侍者和侍从对文学名人根本一无所知。这话他没敢和女王说。

尽管女王与这些当代作家的聚会非常失败，但这次经历并没有像凯文爵士希望的那样导致女王放弃读书。女王再也不想会见作家，甚至在某种程度上对当代作家和他们的作品都失去了兴趣。这意味着她有更多的时间阅读古典名著，阅读狄更斯、萨克雷、乔治·艾略特和勃朗特姐妹的作品。

$$\cdots$$

每周二女王都要与首相会面。一般首相会向她报告一下相关的情况。媒体喜欢将会面描绘成这样：一位富有智慧和经验的君主指引首相规避可能的困难，她那五十年来积累的独特政治经验足以给予首相各种忠告。王室默认了这样的说法。然而，这并不是事实，实际上，随着首相们任职日久，他们听得越来越少，说得越来越多。女王时常只能频频点头，虽然对首相说的并不认同。

在一开始，首相们都希望女王会给他们指引。当他们来见女王的时候，她会鼓励他们一下，就像孩子向母亲展示自己的成就时，母亲会做的那样。对女王而言，这样的会面通常不过是场必需的表演，显示她对首相的兴趣和关心。男人（包括撒切尔夫人）都喜欢表演。在这个阶段，首相们还是会倾听女王的谈话，甚至询问她的建议，但随着时间流逝，这些人全都一致地变成来说教的了。他们一旦不再需要女王的鼓励，而仅仅把她作为一个听众，就不听她的了。这让女王有点不快。

不止一个人像格莱斯顿那样把和女王的会面当成一次公共演说。

今天的会面自然还是这样的套路，直到快结束的时候女王才找到个机会开口，谈起她真正感兴趣的话题。"我想谈谈我的圣诞讲话。"

"有什么问题吗，陛下？"首相问。

"我想今年有所不同。"

"不同？"

"对。我可以坐在沙发上读我的讲话。或者还可以更加随便一点，镜头先拍我在沙发上看书，然后慢慢推进——是这么说吧？——直到我出现在镜头正中。这时我可以抬起头来说：'我一直在看这本关于什么什么的书。'然后开始我的讲话。"

"那会是本什么书呢，陛下？"首相看起来有点不高兴。

"那我还要想一想。"

"也许是关于国际形势的？"首相露出了喜色。

"这也可以考虑，不过报纸上这些消息够多的了。我其实想的是诗歌。"

"诗歌，陛下？"首相勉强笑着。

"比如托马斯·哈代。我读过他的一首好诗。写的是泰坦尼克号与撞沉它的冰山如何融合在一起的。诗的名字叫《会合》。你读过吗？"

"没有，陛下。不过，这会有帮助吗？"

"帮助谁？"

"嗯，"首相似乎觉得有点尴尬地说，"民众。"

"当然了，"女王说，"这首诗说明命运是我们谁都无法逃避的，对吧？"

她说完看着首相，善意地微笑着。

他低着头，看着自己的手说："我想政府也许不能认同这样的观点。"不能让公众觉得世界已经失去了控制。那意味着社会混乱，或是选举失利。对首相来说，这两个结果都一样。

"我听说"——现在轮到首相来善意地微笑了——"陛下访问南非的时候拍的录像很好。"

女王叹了口气，按下了铃。"我们再考虑吧。"

首相知道这意味着会面的结束。诺曼打开门等着。首相心里说："这就是那个出名的诺曼了。"

"哦，诺曼，"女王说，"首相似乎没读过哈代的作品。你送他出去的时候，找一本旧的平装本哈代小说送给他。"

让女王有点惊喜的是，她勉强按自己的想法发表了圣诞讲话。她并没有坐在沙发上，而是像以往一样坐在她的桌子后面，哈代的诗歌也因为不够"积极向上"而没有读成，但她的讲话引用了《双城记》的开头段落："这是最好的时代，也是最坏的时代。"效果不错。女王没有从自动提词机上读这段话，而是直接从书上读的。这让占听众大多数的老年人想起了他们上学时给他们读这本书的老师。

女王从圣诞讲话的反响中受到了鼓舞，因此打算继续坚持在公众场合朗读。一天夜里，她读完关于伊丽莎白宗教和解历史的书后，忽然想到给坎特伯雷大主教打电话。

大主教先调小了电视机的音量，然后才和女王说话。

"大主教。我为什么从来没有读过日课？"

"您什么意思，陛下？"

"在教堂。每个人都有机会朗读一段圣经，而我从来没有读过。没规定说我不可以读吧？我读也可以吧？"

"应该可以吧，陛下。"

"很好。这样的话我就要开始读了。先读《利未记》。晚安。"

大主教摇摇头，继续看电视上的《舞动奇迹》。

不过从此之后，女王经常在教堂读日课，特别是她在诺福克的时候。甚至在苏格兰的时候也这样。不仅这样，参观小学的时候，她坐在教室里为孩子们读一篇小象巴贝（Babar）的故事；而参加伦敦城晚宴时，她朗诵了一首贝奇曼[1]的诗。女王的即兴发挥让所有在场的人都欣喜不已。只有凯文爵士例外。女王事先根本就没有和他商量过这些。

另一场即兴朗诵是在一次植树典礼结束的时候。那是在梅德韦市内一处贫瘠的农场，女王轻松地在刚开垦的土地上种了一棵橡树苗。她一面靠着铁锹休息，一面背诵了菲利普·拉金的诗《树》的最后一段：

---

1 约翰·贝奇曼（Sir John Betjeman，1906—1984），英国诗人、作家、广播节目主持人，从 1972 年起任英国桂冠诗人。

但每个五月这不安分的城堡

枝繁叶茂仍在不停舞动。

去年已逝去，他们似乎是说，

开始重新来，重新来，重新来。

女王的声音清晰无误地回荡在稀疏的草地上，这首诗似乎不仅是给这群市政官员听的，更是为她自己而念。女王感触的是自己的生活，是她生活中的新"开始"。

女王自己也没有想到，爱上读书之后，她会对其他事情失去兴趣。当然，她从不会因为要替游泳池剪彩而激动，但以前她也不反感。不管她的职责有多乏味——参观这里那里，授予这个那个的——她从未觉得厌倦。这些是她的本分。每天早上她翻开记事本时，总是充满兴趣和期待。

现在可不是这样了。女王的各种持续不断的参观、旅行和工作，已经安排到几年之后。浏览这些的时候她只觉得头疼。她几乎没有一天可以自由支配的时间。忽然之间，一切都变得毫无乐趣。听到女王在办公桌后发出的叹息，女仆说："陛下累了。您应该偶尔放松一下。"

女王并不是累了。是因为读书。虽然她热爱读书，但有时她希望自己从没读过书，从没了解过他人的生活。读书把她宠坏了。或者说，读书让她对其他事情失去了兴趣。

···

与此同时，王宫有不少贵客来访，其中之一就是法国总统。和他关于热内的谈话真是令人失望。在国事访问后和外交部长例行的说明会上，女王和他提到了这一点。外交部长也没有听说过热内这位剧作家兼罪犯。女王没有怎么谈法国总统关于英美货币体系的看法，而是接着说，尽管总统对热内一无所知，认为他不过是个住在台球房里的人，但他对普鲁斯特却知之甚深。女王之前只听过普鲁斯特这个名字，没有读过他的书。外交部长连这个名字也没听过，因此女王给他上了一课。

"普鲁斯特的生活很不幸，是个可怜人。他一直受哮喘的困扰。是那种人们看到会说'唉，加把劲吧'的人。不过文学界都是这种人。有意思的是，当他将蛋糕蘸进茶里的时候，他看到了自己过去的生活。这个习惯令人厌恶。嗯，我也试了一次，但毫无效果。我小时候最喜欢的是富勒氏的蛋糕。如果让我吃上一块的话，也许会有点效果。但富勒氏早就已经倒闭了，所以也不会有回忆了。我们可以结束了吧？"女王的手伸向了身旁的书。

与外交部长不同，女王对普鲁斯特的忽视很快就被纠正了。诺曼在网上查找普鲁斯特的资料，发现《追忆似水年华》有十三卷，觉得正适合女王夏天去苏格兰的巴尔莫勒尔堡度假时读，就帮女王借来了。诺曼还一块儿借了乔治·佩因特（George Painter）写的普鲁斯特传记。看着书桌上一字排开的蓝粉色书册，女王觉得它们看起来像刚从糕点店里出来的，似乎可以吃上一口。

这个夏天糟透了。又冷又湿，毫无收获。出门打猎的人每晚回来都会抱怨猎物太少。然而，对女王和诺曼来说，却像田园诗一般美好。书中的世界和他们身边的世界反差太大了。一面是他们两人沉醉的世界：痛苦的斯万，无聊庸俗的维尔迪兰夫人和古怪的德·夏尔吕斯男爵；一面是打猎的人在湿漉漉的山上吹着无味的归营号，偶尔可以看见他们扛着湿透的死牡鹿经过窗外。

根据规定，首相夫妇需要和王室一起度几天假。首相本人不擅狩猎，但他希望至少有机会可以陪女王在荒原上走走。用他的话来说，就是"希望可以更好地了解女王"。可是，首相对普鲁斯特和哈代同样一无所知，所以他只有失望了：计划中的谈心根本没有实现。

早餐之后，女王就和诺曼去书房读书。虽然每天收获不大，王室男丁还是在早餐后开着越野车去狩猎。首相夫妇就只有自己找乐子了。有些时候，他们会无精打采地穿过荒原，走过沼地去和狩猎的人一起在雨中吃顿尴尬的野餐。下午要难打发些。他们已经把周围逛遍了，还买了一条粗花呢毯子和一盒饼干。除此之外，也没有什么可买的了。有时他们只好两人幽怨地在客厅的角落里玩大富翁游戏。

这样过了四天，首相夫妇受够了，决定提早离开。他找了个借口，说是"中东发生了危机"。在他们离开的晚上，大家匆忙组织了一场看手势猜字谜的游戏。女王不为人知的特权之一就是挑选游戏的谜底。一般游戏的谜底都是大家熟知的短语和名言。但女王这次挑选的短语和名言让其他人，包括首相都摸不着头脑。

首相从来不喜欢失败。哪怕是输给女王也不行。一个王子告诉他，除了女王没人能赢，因为题目是诺曼定的，全部来自他和女王读的书，其中还有好几个关于普鲁斯特的。这让他更生气了。

女王这次重新使用她久已放弃的一项君主特权，让首相前所未有地愤怒。一回到伦敦，他马上就让他的特别顾问去找凯文爵士。凯文爵士对首相的遭遇深表同情。他对特别顾问说，诺曼现在是他俩共同的问题。特别顾问不动声色地问："这个叫诺曼的家伙是个同性恋吗？"

凯文爵士不是十分确定，但他认为很有可能。

"那她知道吗？"

"女王陛下？也许吧。"

"那媒体呢？"

"我认为决不能让媒体知道。"凯文爵士说着脸颊抽动了一下。

"正是如此。那你能解决这件事吗？"

碰巧女王接下来要去加拿大进行国事访问。诺曼资格不够，无法随行，就回家乡第斯河畔的斯托克顿度假去了。不过，他在女王出发前已经细心安排好一大箱书，足够女王在横穿加拿大的旅程中读了。就诺曼所知，加拿大人不怎么爱看书，而女王的日程安排得很紧，根本没有时间去书店。女王对这次旅行十分期待。因为要坐很长时间的火车，所以她想象着当火车在美洲大陆上飞驰时，自己可以心无旁骛地读着佩皮斯[1]的书。真是太幸福了！

事实恰恰相反。旅行一开始就不顺。女王心情烦躁，闷闷不乐。原本宫廷侍从可以将这都归结为女王的阅读，但这次却不是这样。女王根本无书可读。诺曼为她准备的书神秘地失踪了。这些书和王室成员一起从希思罗机场出发，却在几个月后出现在卡尔加里的图书馆里，成为一次有点怪异的展览的焦点。凯文爵士特地这么安排是希望女王能将精力都投入到工作中。他的想法没能实现。女王没有书读，不须思考，这让她变得脾气不好，难以相处。

去北方参观时，本来为女王安排了几只北极熊来观

1　塞缪尔·佩皮斯（Samuel Pepys，1633—1703），英国作家、政治家、海军大臣，以流传后世的《佩皮斯日记》闻名。

赏，但她却没有出现。原本在四周晃荡的北极熊纷纷跳上浮冰离开。无论是在海上漂浮拥堵的原木，还是滑入冰冷海水的冰山，女王全都不屑一顾，压根就没有出过船舱门。

"你不想看看圣劳伦斯航道[1]吗？"公爵问她。

"五十年前是我给它开通剪的彩。它肯定还是老样子。"

女王马马虎虎地看了一下洛基山脉，而尼亚加拉瀑布就根本没去。她说："这瀑布我已经看过三次了。"结果公爵只好自己一个人去。

在一次为加拿大文化名人举行的招待会上，女王偶然与爱丽丝·门罗攀谈起来。得知门罗是位作家后，就要了一本她的作品。读过之后，女王十分喜爱。更让女王高兴的是，门罗写过很多书，并且欣然答应全部都送给她。

女王悄悄地问坐在身边的加拿大对外贸易部长："如果你见到一位自己喜欢的作家，而且发现她不只写了你

1　圣劳伦斯航道（St Lawrence Seaway），北美洲五大湖人工航道系统，美国、加拿大联合设计，1959 年建成。

64

读的那一两本书，还写了另外十几本，这是不是最让人高兴的事？"

她没告诉部长，这些书还都是平装本，放在手提包里正合适。女王立刻给诺曼寄了张明信片，让他去图书馆借门罗那几本绝版的书，这样她一回国就可以读。女王觉得这真是人生乐事！

但诺曼没有收到这张明信片。

•••

在诺曼准备出发去第斯河畔的斯托克顿度假的前一天，凯文爵士把他叫到办公室。首相的特别顾问说过，应该解雇诺曼。凯文爵士不喜欢这位特别顾问。虽然他也不喜欢诺曼，但他更不喜欢特别顾问。就是因为这样诺曼才没有被解雇。此外，凯文爵士觉得解雇这个办法有点低级。不需要解雇诺曼。他还有更好的办法。

他对诺曼亲切地说："女王陛下一向关心雇员的发展。她对你的工作十分满意，但她想知道你是否考虑过上大学？"

"上大学？"诺曼问道。他从没考虑过这个问题。

"具体地说是东安格利亚大学。他们的英文系非常好，写作学院也很棒。我只要提几个名字——"凯文爵士低头看他的记事簿，"比如伊恩·麦克尤恩，罗丝·特里梅因[1]和石黑一雄……"

"嗯，"诺曼说，"这些作家的作品我们都读过。"

"我们"这个字眼让女王的私人秘书停顿了一下，然后他接着说，他认为东安格利亚大学很适合诺曼。

"为什么呢？"诺曼问。"我又没有钱。"

"这不是问题。你知道，女王陛下希望你能得到很好的发展。"

"我想我还是愿意留在这里，"诺曼说，"在这里就像在上大学一样。"

"是——吗？"凯文爵士说。"那不可能。陛下已经有别的人选来接替你的工作了。"

他善意地笑着说："当然了，你在厨房的工作随时欢迎你回去。"

1　罗丝·特里梅因（Rose Tremain，1943— ），英国作家，现为东安格利亚大学校长。

这样，当女王从加拿大回来的时候，诺曼已经在王宫里消失了。走廊里原来他坐的椅子不见了，一直堆在女王床头的书也没了。最直接的影响是，她没有人可以一起谈论爱丽丝·门罗了。

"他不怎么招人喜欢，陛下。"凯文爵士告诉她。

"我喜欢他，"女王回答，"他去哪里了？"

"不知道，陛下。"

诺曼是个敏感的男孩子。离开王宫后，他给女王写过一封长信，告诉她自己学习的课程以及阅读的书。当他收到一封开头是"谢谢你的来信，女王对此很感兴趣"的回信时，他知道自己已经被不动声色地赶出了王宫。他只是不清楚这究竟是女王的意思，还是她的私人秘书做的。

女王心里对这件事十分明白。诺曼离开的原因和流动图书馆消失以及书会送到卡尔加里的原因是一样的。从某种意义上来说，诺曼就像那天她藏在马车垫子下面的那本书。不过他的运气好，没有被炸掉。当然，女王很想念诺曼。可是他从不给她写信，连只字片语也没有。女王也没有别的办法，只有坚强地独自继续下去。诺曼的离去是不会让她停止读书的。

女王并没有被诺曼的突然离去所困扰。这似乎有点异乎寻常，也难免让人对她的性格有些微词。不过，女王的一生中有无数的人意外失踪或突然离去。比方说，人们一般不会告诉她有人生病的事。作为女王，她不需要悲伤，甚至也不需要同情心。至少她的臣子们是这样想的。女王往往要到这不幸的仆人或朋友去世时，才第一次听到他们生病的消息。对所有的仆人来说，"不要让女王陛下担心"是不变的金科玉律。

　　当然，诺曼没有死，只是去了东安格利亚大学。可在宫廷侍从们看来，这没什么不同。因为他已经从女王的生活中消失了，也就从此不存在了。无论是女王还是别人都没再提过诺曼的名字。侍从们认为女王这样做是对的，没有什么可指责的。有人去世，有人离开，还有越来越多的人进入了故纸堆。对女王来说，这些都不过是各种各样的离去。这些人都离开了，而她还要继续生活。

　　在诺曼神秘离开以前，女王已经开始思考，自己是否已经超越了他，或者说在读书方面超过他了。这一点可能不会让侍从们赞赏。诺曼一度谦恭但直接地引导着女王的阅读。他对女王应该读什么书提出建议，还会毫不犹豫地告诉她，哪些书还不适合她读。比如，他一直没让她读贝克特和纳博科夫。菲利普·罗斯[1]的书也是慢慢地一本一本地介绍给她的，特地将《波特诺伊的怨诉》放在后面让她读。

渐渐地，女王和诺曼把他们想读的书几乎都读了。当他们一起谈论自己在读的书时，女王越来越觉得自己的生活经历让自己的理解比诺曼要深刻。书籍能给的其实有限。她还发现，诺曼的品位有时候也并不可信。在同等条件下，他总是倾向于喜欢同性的作家。因此她才会读到热内的作品。这些作家有些女王喜欢，比如玛丽·瑞瑙特[2]的小说就让她着迷；有些女王觉得是在进行变态的说教，比如诺曼喜欢的丹顿·韦尔奇[3]，她就觉得

---

1 菲利普·罗斯（Philip Roth，1933— ），20世纪美国最具代表性的犹太作家，长篇小说《波特诺伊的怨诉》因其中描写的性意识引发较多争议。

2 玛丽·瑞瑙特（Mary Renault，1905—1983），英国历史小说家，作品多取材于古希腊时期，关注同性爱并广泛探讨伦理和哲学问题，深入审视爱和权力的本质，代表作"亚历山大三部曲"。

3 丹顿·韦尔奇（Denton Welch，1915—1948），英国作家、画家，以文笔细腻动人著称。韦尔奇的同性恋倾向也是受人关注的话题。

他的作品不健康；还有依舍伍德[1]，他作品中的冥想实在太多了。作为一名读者，女王是活泼坦率的。她不想沉溺于某个方面。

因为没有诺曼一起讨论，女王开始和自己长篇大论地探讨问题，记下的想法越来越多，笔记本不断增加，涉及的领域也更广泛。"要得到幸福，就不能认为得到它是理所当然的。"她在这句话旁加了颗星，还在页尾写道："我从来不曾知道这个道理。"

"有一次在授予荣誉勋爵的时候，我记得是安东尼·鲍威尔[2]，我们谈到了不雅举止。他自己举止优雅，甚至有些传统。他说，作为作家不能不食人间烟火。不过女王却可以（我没有对他这样说）。我可能看上去不是这样，但其实一直都是不食人间烟火的。我有人替我做。"

1 克里斯托弗·依舍伍德（Christopher Isherwood，1904—1986），英国小说家、剧作家，作品带有浓厚的自传色彩。1946 年加入美国籍，后期经历精神上的蜕变，从早年的左倾、热心政治转向印度吠檀多派的清心寡欲。
2 安东尼·鲍威尔（Anthony Powell，1905—2000），小说家，被称为"英国的普鲁斯特"，代表作为长达十二卷本的小说《时光曲之舞》，1951 年到 1975 年间出版。

除了这些思考之外，女王还开始在笔记中描摹她见过的人。这些人并不都是名人。她记下他们举止的怪异之处，语言的独特方面，还有他们悄悄告诉她的故事。当报纸上出现关于王室的不实报道时，女王在笔记中记下真实的情况；当有些流言蜚语逃过公众的关注时，女王同样也在笔记中记上一笔。所有这些记录的语气都是理性而务实的。女王意识到这就是自己的风格，不由得有些欣喜。

诺曼离开后，虽然女王没有停止读书，但的确有了变化。女王依然还是从伦敦图书馆借书，从书店买书。诺曼不在了，这就不再是他们两人之间的小秘密了。女王要让宫廷女侍去找王室审计员，才能提出一点钱去买书。这个过程让女王十分厌烦，所以有时候她会绕过它，请某个不怎么亲近的孙辈帮她买书。他们通常都很高兴帮忙。女王能留意到他们已经够让他们开心的了。一般公众都不知道他们的存在。不过，女王开始更为频繁地借阅自己的图书馆，特别是温莎图书馆里的书。温莎图书馆里的现当代书籍虽然不够全，但书架上全是各种版本的经典作品，其中不少还有作者的签名。她开始读巴尔扎克、屠格涅夫、菲尔丁和康拉德的作品。这些她以前认为太难的书，现在读起来如鱼得水。读书的时候她总是手里拿着铅笔，准备做笔记。女王在阅读这些经典作品的过程中，居然也顺便原谅了亨利·詹姆斯，对他的散漫泰然自若。她在笔记本上写道："毕竟，不是所有的小说都要写成平铺直叙的。"看见女王坐在窗户边用黄昏最后的一丝光线看书，图书管理员感叹，在这座古老的图书馆里，自从乔治三世[1]以来，可能就没有比她更勤勉的读者了。

与许多人一样，温莎图书馆的管理员也向女王竭力推荐简·奥斯丁。这么多人都同样地说女王会如何喜欢奥斯丁，这反而让她提不起兴趣。此外，作为简·奥斯丁的读者，由于女王的特殊身份，她还有难以解决的问题。奥斯丁作品的精髓在于对社会的阶层差别准确而微妙的呈现。处在女王这样的地位，她很难理解这种微妙的社会差别。君主与臣子之间存在的巨大差异远超过奥

1　乔治三世（1738—1820），英国国王，汉诺威王朝的第三位不列颠君　主，维多利亚女王的祖父，统治期间经历了英法七年战争、北美殖　民地独立、击败拿破仑等重大历史事件。乔治三世一生酷爱书籍，　拥有超过六万卷私人藏书，1823 年其子乔治四世将他的书捐赠给大　英图书馆，即著名的"国王藏书"。

斯丁小说中的社会差别。比起普通读者，女王认为奥斯丁刻意呈现的社会差别并不重要。因此她觉得这些小说很难读下去。对这位王室读者来说，简·奥斯丁的作品几乎就是昆虫学研究，小说中的人物虽然不是全都像蚂蚁那么大，至少也小得需要一台显微镜才能看得清。直到女王不仅理解了文学，而且认识了人性之后，她才意识到这些人物的个性和魅力。

出于同样的原因，女王也轻视过女性主义。比起女王与其他人之间的巨大鸿沟来说，性别差异和阶级差别一样都无足轻重。

女王最终不仅阅读了简·奥斯丁和女性主义作品，甚至还读了陀斯妥耶夫斯基和很多其他的文学作品。阅读过程中她不乏遗憾。多年之前，女王曾与大卫·塞西尔[1]勋爵在牛津的一次晚宴上比邻而坐。那时两人几乎无话可说。现在她发现大卫勋爵写过几本关于简·奥斯丁的书，如果两人此时见面的话，一定会谈得津津有味。

---

1 大卫·塞西尔（David Cecil，1902—1986），英国传记作家、历史学家和学者，著有《简·奥斯丁画像》。

可是大卫勋爵已经去世了。太晚了。真是太晚了。一切都太晚了。不过，女王依然怀着希望，坚持继续阅读下去，希望能够弥补失去的时间。

•••

整个王室依然平稳地运转着。从伦敦到温莎，从诺福克到苏格兰，毫不需要女王费心。有时她甚至觉得自己有点多余。不管中心人物是谁，同样的变动还是会顺利完成的。她不过是出发与抵达的例行仪式上的一件行李。虽然没有人会质疑她的重要性，但毕竟还是一件行李。

从某个方面来说，这些游历比以往更为成功，因为中心人物女王一般总是在看书。她在白金汉宫上了车，一路到温莎都在读克罗奇贝克上尉在克里特的大撤离。在飞往苏格兰的路上，她高兴（有时是生气）地读着《项狄传》。读烦了就改读特罗洛普（名叫安东尼那位）[1]。

1　安东尼·特罗洛普（Anthony Trollope，1815—1882），英国维多利亚时期最为成功、多产和受人尊敬的小说家之一，代表作为"巴塞特郡"系列长篇小说。艾伦·贝内特曾评价"较之萨克雷和狄更斯，他笔下维多利亚时代的世俗生活画面写得更确切、多样和全面"。

这让女王在旅行的时候和蔼顺从，要求不高。不过，她没有以往准时了。在院子里的天篷下，公爵经常焦躁不安地坐在车里等她。当女王最后终于匆匆上了车，她从不烦躁：毕竟，她拿着书呢。

其他人却感受不到这样的慰藉。尤其是王室侍从，他们对女王的表现越来越不耐烦，开始说三道四。侍从们举止优雅，彬彬有礼，但实质上就犹如舞台监督。他们明白自己要表现得恭顺，但很清楚这一切不过是一场演出：女王是主角，他们才是演出负责人。

有女王的地方，人人都是观众。这些观众虽然明知一切不过是场表演，但并不愿意承认事实，而且认为，就算是表演，他们偶尔也会在其中看到一些更"自然"、更"真实"的东西。比如说，无意中听到的古怪谈话。女王的母亲晚年时说的那句"我会杀死一杯金托尼酒。"还有爱丁堡公爵说过的"该死的狗"！再比如说，看到女王在花园酒会上一坐下来就高兴地脱掉鞋子。实际上，这些所谓的非表演瞬间一样是事先安排好的。王室成员从来都是一丝不苟的。这类表演，或者说串场，演的就是作为普通人的王室。和王室成员在公众场合的正式表演一样都是设计好的。不过，那些听到这些话，看到这些事的人会把这类表演当做女王和王室成员最人性化、最自然的时候。无论是否在正式场合，所有的一切都是在王室侍从的协助下展现一种形象。除了那些明显的即兴表演之外，看起来全都天衣无缝。

侍从们渐渐留意到，女王这些所谓真实的瞬间出现得越来越少了。尽管她依然勤勉地完成自己的职责，但除此之外，她再也不会像从前那样扮出放松的样子，也不再说一些貌似即兴的话。比如过去有一次，在给一位青年戴上勋章时，女王说了一句："小心点，我可不想刺穿你的心。"这些话让人印象深刻，十分难忘。和王室请柬、特别停车证以及王宫地图一样，都是人们记忆的一部分。

现在的女王有些一本正经，笑容貌似真挚但总让人觉得有些虚假，而且她也不说那些即兴的闲话了。以往这些闲话总能让仪式变得活泼些。"真是乏味的表演。"宫廷侍从们这么想。他们认为现在所有的表演都如此乏味，因为女王的表现实在不够生动。以前都是侍从们与女王合作，才使得那些所谓真实的瞬间看来自然天成，成为女王幽默感的真实流露。现在他们自然不能让别人注意到女王的变化。

在一次就职仪式后，一位胆子比较大的侍从对女王说："陛下，您今天早晨表现得不够自然。"

"是吗？"女王说。以往，哪怕一点点温和的批评也会让她不安，现在她却处之泰然。"我想可能是这样的。杰拉德，你知道当他们跪下来的时候，我大部分时间都在看他们的头顶。看着那些开始秃颓的发际和领子外的长发，即使最冷漠的人也会感到同情。我几乎有种母性的冲动。"

女王从来没有和侍从说过这样的私房话。说来他本该感到荣幸，但他却觉得十分尴尬。这才真正是女王人性的一面。他从没有意识到这一点。他更喜欢以前那些表演。女王觉得自己这种情感的流露可能来自读书，而侍从觉得这也许是她年老的征兆。情感的勃发却被当成了衰老的肇始。

女王从不会觉得尴尬，也从不会留意别人的尴尬。如果是以前，她根本不会发现这位年轻侍从的神态有异。现在，既然她注意到了这一点，就决定以后不再这样随便地表露自己的想法。这个决定真是太可惜了，因为许多人都盼着能了解女王的思想。她决定只把自己的思考写在笔记本里。那不会引起任何麻烦。

女王从不公开表露自己的感情。她接受的教育就是这样。然而，近来，特别是戴安娜王妃去世后的那段时间，虽然她并不愿意，却不得不在公开场合表达自己的感情。那时，女王还没有读书的习惯。现在，她明白自己的困境并非独一无二。还有很多人，比如考迪里亚[1]，也和她一样。女王在笔记本中写道："虽然我对莎士比亚不是那么了解，但我完全赞同考迪里亚的那句'我不会用我的嘴来表达我的心'。她的处境和我一样。"

女王对记笔记这件事一直都很谨慎，但她的贴身侍从并不放心。他看到过一两次，认为这可能是女王精神不稳定的表现。女王陛下要记什么呢？她以前从不这样。对上了年纪的人来说，行为的突然改变就意味着衰老的加速。

"也许是老年痴呆症，"另一个侍从说，"要把所有

1　莎士比亚悲剧《李尔王》中李尔的小女儿。

的事情都写下来，就是这样吧？"这些揣测加上女王对自己的外表越来越不关心，让她身边的扈从们担心不已。

毫无疑问，从人性和同情的角度出发，女王可能得了老年痴呆症的确让人震惊。对杰拉德和其他侍从来说，更是觉得万分遗憾。在杰拉德看来，女王的生活一向是深居简出，与众不同的，现在却和不少平民一样得了这样不体面的病。他觉得，女王的衰老应该有王室独特的风范，应该具有君主的气质，在得老年痴呆症之前，要有些不同凡响的行为举止才对。如果杰拉德知道三段论的话，他肯定会这么说：老年痴呆症是普通人的病，女王不是普通人，所以女王不会得老年痴呆症。

当然，女王根本就没得老年痴呆症。事实上，她的能力比以往更强。与她的侍从不一样，她清楚地知道什么是三段论。

除了记笔记和习惯性的迟到之外，女王还有什么衰老的迹象呢？现在女王会接连两天戴同一枚胸针，穿同一双鞋子。其实，原因是她根本不在乎，或者说不像以往那么在乎这些了。一旦女王自己不在乎，她的侍从也就不那么在乎了，一般都草草了事。这大概也是人性的弱点。以前女王是不可能允许这样的情况发生的。她一直极为在意自己的衣着，对自己的衣服和配饰了如指掌，总是细心地搭配和更换。现在她变了。普通的女性如果两周穿同一件外衣，可能没人会说她过于随便，不修边幅。可是，对衣着从来一丝不苟的女王来说，这样的现象说明她完全背弃了自己一直严格遵守的高雅标准。

"陛下难道不在意吗？"女仆大胆地说了一句。

"在意什么？"女王说。这回答没有让女仆放心，反而使她确信肯定是出了严重的问题。和宫廷侍从一样，女王的贴身仆人也开始认为这是女王漫长衰老的开始。

•••

不过，虽然每周都和女王见面，首相却没有注意到女王现在不常换衣服，还常戴着同一副耳环。

以前不是这样的。首相刚上台的时候，他时常夸赞女王的衣着和首饰高雅得体。当然，那时他的年纪还没有这么大，觉得这样说是暧昧的讨好。其实那不过是首相紧张的表现罢了。女王那时自然也没有现在这么大年纪，但她可不紧张。她对这一套已经很熟悉了，知道这不过是大多数首相们（除了希思首相和撒切尔夫人）都会经过的一个阶段。随着他们对会面新鲜感的消逝，这种暧昧的讨好也不会再有。

这就是关于女王和首相的另一个有趣的方面。首相对女王外貌的关注度和对女王说话的关注度是一致的。随着时间流逝，女王的外貌和女王的想法对首相而言都不再重要。因此，女王戴不戴耳环，首相根本无所谓。女王偶尔说上两句的时候，觉得自己就像飞机上的空乘在给乘客讲解安全知识，首相脸上那善意而淡漠的样子就像已经听过这些讲解无数次的乘客。

女王同样对他们的会面有点淡漠，或者说，厌烦。她读的书越来越多，而这样的会面花去了不少时间。这让女王颇为不平。她想，也许可以将会面和自己读的书、研究的历史结合起来，这样可能会更有趣一些。

这个想法没有起到作用。首相从不相信历史，也不认为能从历史中得到任何教益。一天晚上，在他和女王谈论中东问题的时候，女王试着说了一句："那里可是人类文明的摇篮呀。"

首相回答："只要我们坚持下去，它还会再次成为文明的摇篮的，陛下。"然后就赶紧改变话题，谈起在那里已经铺设的新下水管道和设立的变电站。

女王再次打断他："我希望这样做不会破坏古迹。你听说过乌尔城[1]吗？"

首相从没听过。他离开的时候，女王送了他几本书，好让他了解一下中东的历史。下一周他们会面的时候，女王问首相有没有读过这些书。虽然他根本没读，但还是回答："这些书都很有意思，陛下。"

"好，这样的话我再找几本给你。我觉得那里的历史有趣极了。"

这次女王感兴趣的是伊朗。她问首相是否了解波斯或伊朗的历史，然后就给了他一本书。首相之前一直以为波斯和伊朗是两个不相干的名称。从此每次会面女王基本都会这么做。以前首相把周二晚上的会面当做一周繁忙工作中的一个放松。可是，两三次讨论历史的会面之后，首相再也没有轻松的感觉了，反而对每次会面都

1　乌尔城，美索不达米亚古代城市，位于今伊拉克的穆盖伊尔。该城历史可以追溯至公元前约 3800 年，公元前 26 世纪发展为苏美尔人的城邦国家。

充满了忧虑。女王甚至还会像检查作业一样，向他提问，发现他根本没看书时，总是宽容地笑笑。

"首相先生，根据我的了解，除了麦克米兰先生[1]之外，首相们都喜欢让别人帮他们读书。"

"我很忙，陛下。"首相回答。

"我也很忙。"女王附和着，同时手伸向了一本书。"我们下周再见吧。"

终于凯文爵士接到了来自首相特别顾问的电话。

"你的老板在为难我的老板。"

"是吗？"

"就是这样。不停地借书给他读。这样不行。"

"女王陛下喜欢读书。"

"我还喜欢有人给我吹箫呢。但我不会让首相这么做。凯文，你有办法吗？"

"我会和陛下谈一谈的。"

"凯文，就这么说了。告诉她别再借书给我老板了。"

1　指哈罗德·麦克米兰（Harold Macmillan，1894—1986），第一代斯托克顿伯爵，英国保守党政治家，于 1957 至 1963 年期间出任英国首相。

凯文爵士没有和女王谈这个问题，更没有让她别再借书给首相，而是放弃了自尊，去找克劳德爵士。

•••

克劳德·波林顿爵士的住所是一座十七世纪建造的乡间小屋。小屋十分漂亮，就在汉普顿区。此刻他正在自己的小花园里阅读。准确地说，克劳德爵士是打算阅读，因为实际上他正在打瞌睡。他的身边搁着一盒温莎图书馆送来的机密文件。这是资深王室仆人才有的特权。虽然克劳德爵士至少已经有九十岁了，但还在装模作样地在写着自己的回忆录。他给回忆录起的题目叫《苦工里的圣人》。

克劳德爵士十八岁的时候离开家乡哈罗镇，加入王室仆从的队伍，成为暴躁而严谨的乔治五世的侍童。他喜欢回忆当时做的第一件差使，就是为这位国王的集邮册舔用来粘邮票的透明玻璃纸。在接受苏·劳利[1]访问的

1　苏·劳利（Sue Lawley），英国著名媒体人，曾在 BBC、ITV 等机构工作，在节目中采访过王室成员和梅杰首相。

84

时候，克劳德爵士曾说："要找我的 DNA 一点都不难。只要在王室集邮册里那些邮票后面找就行了。那些图瓦邮票[1] 我记得最清楚。国王陛下觉得它们太普通了，而且有些低俗，但他认为必须要收集。他就是这样：有时候过于严谨，这就是他的缺点。"那次节目中他选放的歌曲是欧内斯特·洛夫唱的《鸽翼颂》。[2]

在克劳德爵士不大的客厅里，到处都放着他和曾经服务过的王室成员的照片。有他在爱斯科赛马场上，帮乔治五世拿着望远镜的照片，也有他匍匐在荒原上，身边的乔治五世正拿枪瞄准远处牡鹿的照片。还有他跟着玛丽王后从哈里盖特的古董店出来的照片。照片里年轻的克劳德爵士的脸被一个装着韦奇伍德花瓶的包裹遮住了。那个花瓶是一个倒霉的商人很不情愿地送给玛丽王后的。[3] 当然，还有他穿着条纹运动衫，在"纳林号"那次地中海之行上充当船员的照片。这次航行改变了很多

1　图瓦是生活在中亚的一个民族，20 世纪二三十年代发行过图瓦主题的邮票，因为独特的异域色彩得到当时不少西方人的青睐。

2　欧内斯特·洛夫（Ernest Lough, 1911—2000）是英国著名童声男高音。《鸽翼颂》是其最著名的独唱歌曲，1927 年唱片发行后风靡一时。

3　乔治五世的玛丽王后素以痴迷收藏珠宝古董而闻名。

人的命运。[1]照片中戴着游艇帽的女士就是辛普森夫人。这张照片不时会被收起来。以前女王的母亲常来喝下午茶，克劳德爵士从没让她看到过这张照片。

王室的秘密没有克劳德爵士不知道的。侍奉过乔治五世之后，他又先后侍奉过爱德华八世和他的兄弟乔治六世。他在王室的各个部门都工作过，最后一份工作是女王的私人秘书。尽管克劳德爵士早已退休，但人们还是常来咨询他的意见。他是整个王室交口赞誉的活化石，是一个"十分可靠的人"。

如今，克劳德爵士的手有些发抖，似乎没那么可靠了。现在他对自己的个人卫生也有些马虎，不像过去那么仔细了。虽然坐在芬芳的花园里，凯文爵士还是不得不屏住呼吸。

"我们进屋谈吧？"克劳德爵士说。"可以一起喝点下午茶。"

"不了，不了，"凯文爵士赶紧说，"这里更好。"

---

1 1936年夏，刚继位的英王爱德华八世不顾王室与政府反对，和有夫之妇辛普森夫人乘坐"纳林号"巡游东欧各国。11月，为迎娶辛普森夫人，爱德华八世宣布退位，被封为温莎公爵。

他向克劳德爵士说了女王读书引起的问题。

"读书？"克劳德爵士问。"这没什么坏处吧？女王陛下像与她同名的另一位女王，伊丽莎白一世。那也是位爱读书的人。不过，那时候书还不多。女王陛下的母亲也喜欢书。玛丽王后不喜欢。乔治五世也喜欢读书。他喜欢集邮。我刚开始工作的时候就是为他舔那些粘邮票的透明玻璃纸。"

一个比克劳德爵士年纪还大的仆人为他们端出了下午茶。凯文爵士小心翼翼地倒了一杯。

"克劳德爵士，女王陛下对您十分器重。"

"我也很喜欢她，"克劳德爵士回答，"从她还是个小姑娘的时候，我就开始为她服务。干了整整一辈子。"

他终究还是出人头地的。年轻的波林顿在战争中赢得了勇敢的赞誉和几块勋章，最后进了总参谋部。

克劳德爵士喜欢说："我服务过一位女王、两位王后，和她们都相处得很好。我唯一没法处好的'女王'是陆军元帅蒙哥马利。"[1]

---

1 英文的 queen 除了指女王和王后，还可以指喜欢同性的男子。

"女王听您的话。"凯文爵士一面说，一面想着盘子里的松饼是否能吃。

"我也这么想，"克劳德爵士说，"不过我和她怎么说呢？说她的阅读吗？那太奇怪了。吃块松饼吧。"

凯文爵士及时发现，原来松饼上白色的不是糖霜，而是霉毛。他偷偷地把松饼捏在手上，放进了手提箱。

"也许您可以提醒一下女王她所负有的责任。"

"女王陛下从不需要别人提醒她这一点。如果让我说，她的责任倒是太多了。让我想想……"

老人陷入了沉思。凯文爵士只好等着。

过了好一会儿，他才意识到，克劳德爵士睡着了。凯文爵士站起身来，故意弄出很大的动静。

克劳德爵士醒过来说："我会去见女王的。我有一段时间没有出游了。你会派车来接的吧？"

"那当然了，"凯文爵士和他握手告别，"你不用送了。"

离开的时候，克劳德爵士在他身后喊道："你是那个新西兰人吧？"

···

宫廷侍从对女王说："也许陛下最好在花园里接见克劳德爵士。"

"在花园里？"

"室外的空气比较新鲜，陛下。"

女王看着他说："你的意思是说他身上有臭味？"

"有那么一点，陛下。"

"可怜的人。"她有时会想，这些人根本不知道自己的经历有多丰富。"不行。他必须到这儿来。"

不过，侍从提出要打开窗户的时候，女王没有反对。

"他为什么要见我？"

"不清楚，陛下。"

克劳德爵士拄着两根拐杖进来，在门口就向女王鞠躬致意。女王伸手示意他坐下，他又再次鞠躬致意。虽然女王的微笑依然和蔼，举止依旧可亲，但毫无疑问侍从说的一点也不夸张。

"克劳德爵士，你最近可好？"

"我很好，陛下。您最近可好？"

"我也很好。"

女王等着克劳德爵士开口，但克劳德爵士觉得，作为臣子，不该先开口，所以他等着女王的问话。

"你来见我有什么事吗？"

克劳德爵士努力回想着自己此行的目的。女王注意到他的衣领下积着一层头屑，领带上有鸡蛋留下的污渍，大而下垂的耳朵上还飘荡着皮屑。以往她不会留意到这些，也不会有任何感想。现在她却凝视着这些衰老的细节，失去了一贯的镇定自若，甚至有点不安和伤感。可怜的人。他还在托布鲁克[1]打过仗呢。她要把这个写下来。

"读书，陛下。"

"你说什么？"

"陛下喜欢上读书了。"

"不对，克劳德爵士。我一直都喜欢读书。只不过最近读的书多了一点。"

现在，女王明白他来的目的，也知道是谁让他来的

---

1 托布鲁克（Tobruk），利比亚港口城市，位于地中海东部海岸。1941年4月到11月的托布鲁克围城战是二战北非战场的重要战役，盟军在轴心国军队的包围下坚守这一关键港口240多天。

了。这位曾伴随她左右数十年的老臣，是来找麻烦的。他不再值得怜悯了。女王的同情心一扫而空，恢复了镇定。

"我认为读书本身没有坏处，陛下。"

"我很高兴你这么说。"

"但读得过多就不好了。那就有害了。"

"你是建议我读书要限量吗？"

"陛下是众人的榜样。读书正适合作为您的爱好。如果您对其他的事倾注同样热情的话，可能早就是一片哗然了。"

"也许吧。不过我一直都生活得低调，从未引起过公众哗然。这倒不是自吹自擂。"

"陛下一直喜欢赛马。"

"是的。但是现在我不怎么喜欢。"

"哦，"克劳德爵士说，"太可惜了。"他忽然觉得可以将赛马和读书结合起来，就接着说："女王陛下的母亲以前特别喜欢迪克·弗朗西斯[1]。"

1　迪克·弗朗西斯（Dick Francis，1920—2010），英国骑师、侦探小说作家，大部分作品的主题围绕赛马，曾三次获得美国侦探推理小说家协会最佳小说奖。

"是的，"女王说，"我读过一两本他的书，但比较一般。我发现斯威夫特写马特别出色。[1]"

克劳德爵士黯然地点了点头。不仅是因为他没有读过斯威夫特，更是因为他意识到自己的谈话根本没有效果。

两人沉默了一会。只这一会儿工夫，克劳德爵士已经睡着了。女王很少遇到这种情况。一旦碰到，比如说某个庆典上一个部长在她旁边打瞌睡，她的反应通常都是迅速而不留情面的。女王也经常想打瞌睡。谁来做她的工作都会这样。此时女王却没有叫醒克劳德爵士，而是耐心地等待着。她听着他用力的呼吸声，寻思着再过多久自己会变得这样的老迈，这样的衰弱。女王明白克劳德爵士带来的信息。对此她有些憎恶。不过，也许克劳德爵士本人就是一个信息，向女王预示着一个令人不快的未来。

她拿起桌上的笔记本，丢在地上。克劳德爵士点着头

---

1 斯威夫特《格列佛游记》的"慧骃国游记"中，马是拥有理性的居民和统治者，而人形的"耶胡"则是牲畜。

醒了过来，面带微笑，似乎在赞同女王刚刚说过的一些话。

"你的回忆录写得怎么样了？"女王问他。克劳德爵士的回忆录写的时间太长了，已经成为王室的一个经典笑话。"写到哪一年了？"

"啊，我不是按照年代顺序写的，陛下。我每天都写一点。"

当然，事实并不是这样。不过为了不让女王追问下去，他只好这么说。

"陛下是否有写作计划呢？"

"没有。"女王回答。这也不是实话。"我哪有时间呢？"

"但陛下有时间读书。"

这是在指责女王。她通常对指责不那么宽容，但这次她没在意。

"我应该写什么呢？"

"陛下的生活经历那可是丰富多彩啊。"

"是这样的，"女王说，"我的生活经历的确丰富。"

其实，克劳德爵士完全不懂女王应该写什么，或者她是否应该写作。他这么说，只是为了转移女王对读书的热情。根据他的经验，写作是条死胡同，不会有成果的。克劳德爵士写了二十年的回忆录，还没写完五十页。

"对，"克劳德爵士坚定地说，"陛下一定要写。我能给陛下一点建议吗？不要从一开始写。我就犯了这个错误。从中间开始写。按照年代写总是碍手碍脚的。"

"克劳德爵士，你还有别的事吗？"

女王深深一笑，表示会面结束了。她传达这一讯息的方式总是让克劳德爵士迷惑，但她做得犹如按铃一样明白无误。他站起身来，侍从为他打开门。克劳德爵士向女王鞠了一躬，然后走到门口时又鞠了一躬，才拄着两个拐杖慢慢离去。这两个拐杖中有一个是女王的母亲送给他的。

屋内的女王将窗户开大了一点，好让花园的风吹进来。侍从回来后，惊讶地发现女王指着克劳德爵士刚才坐过的椅子。椅子的绸缎坐垫上有一块水渍。侍从默默地将椅子搬走。女王拿起书和羊毛衫，准备去花园读书。

侍从搬着另一把椅子回来的时候，女王已经走到外面的露台去了。他放下椅子，训练有素地收拾好了房间。这时他看见女王的笔记本在地上。他把它捡了起来，但却没有直接把它放到桌上。他犹豫着，是否可以趁女王不在，偷看一下里面的内容。就在这时，女王忽然出现在门口。

"谢谢你，杰拉德。"她说着伸出了手。

侍从将笔记本交给她后，女王离开了房间。

"糟糕，"杰拉德说，"糟糕！糟糕！糟糕！"

杰拉德的自责无疑是正确的。没几天他就从女王的身边消失，离开了王室，回到他几乎已经忘记的军团，在诺森伯兰郡的荒野中负重跋涉。用凯文爵士的话来说，这种都铎王朝风格的遣送，速度之快，手法之毫不留情，准确地告诉人们：女王还是女王，她并没有衰老。关于女王已经老迈的流言遽然而止。

•••

克劳德爵士的话对女王无足轻重。然而当天晚上，她去皇家阿尔伯特音乐厅，出席一场专门为她举行的逍遥音乐会 [1] 时，却禁不住思考着克劳德爵士说过的话。过

1　逍遥音乐会（promenade concert），每年夏天在伦敦皇家艾尔伯特大厅举行的大型古典音乐节，面向大众，氛围休闲，观众可以站着欣赏音乐会，并可随意走动，犹似散步（promenade）。

去，女王从不觉得音乐是种慰藉，反而更像是种责任。她熟悉的曲目都来自这种不得不参加的音乐会。不过，今晚的音乐似乎正合女王的心意。

她觉得，那个男孩在吹奏单簧管的时候，发出了一种声音。那是莫扎特的声音。虽然莫扎特已经去世两百年了，但音乐厅中的每个人还是能分辨得出这是他的声音。女王记起，E. M. 福斯特在《霍华德庄园》里描述过，海伦·施莱格尔在女王音乐厅的音乐会上，为贝多芬画像。贝多芬的声音也是所有人都熟知的。

男孩演奏完毕，观众和女王一起鼓掌致意。她将身子转向公爵，似乎要与他分享自己的愉悦。其实，她想对他说的是，虽然她年事已长，声望出众，但却没人熟悉她的声音。在返回王宫的车上，女王忽然说了一句："我没有声音。"

"不奇怪，"公爵回答说，"天气太热了。你嗓子不好，是吧？"

这个晚上特别闷热。女王早早地醒来，再也无法入睡。这对她来说，有点不太寻常。

花园中值班的警卫，看到房间里灯亮了，赶紧打开手机，作为预警。

女王最近在读关于勃朗特姐妹的书。她们幼年的生活真是艰辛，但女王觉得继续读下去，她也不会有睡意，就想找点别的书来看。她在书架的角落里看到了那本艾维·康普顿-伯内特的书。那是很久以前她在流动图书馆借的，后来哈钦斯先生把书送给了她。女王记得当时这本书很难卒读，让她昏昏欲睡。现在也许它还有同样的功效。

结果恰恰相反。女王以前觉得这本书节奏缓慢，现在读来却清新生动，虽然还有些枯燥，但却风格明快。艾维夫人严肃的语气与女王自己说话的语气比较接近，读起来十分自然。女王意识到，和其他的不少事情一样，读书就像一块肌肉，而她已经锻炼出来了。这本书女王读来轻松愉快，以往她根本没有留意的一些话（不是笑话）现在让她大笑不已。第二天她把这个感想记了下来。在这本书里，女王可以听到艾维·康普顿-伯内特那理智、严厉而睿智的声音。艾维夫人的声音与音乐会上莫扎特的声音一样的清晰可辨。女王合上书，再次大声地说道："我没有声音。"

在伦敦西区负责监听王室的录音室里，一个面无表情的打字员誊写到这里时，觉得女王的这个说法实在奇怪，忍不住答道："嗨，如果你没有声音的话，我不知道谁还有声音。"

此时，白金汉宫里的女王等了一会，然后关上了灯。梓树下的警卫看到灯灭了，就又关上了手机。

在黑暗之中，女王意识到，去世以后，她将只会活在人们的记忆中。一直高高在上的她将会变得与她的臣民一样。读书无法改变这一点——但写作也许可以。

如果有人问女王，读书是否丰富了她的生活，她会毫不犹豫地点头称是。但她会加上一句，读书同样也让她筋疲力尽。过去，她是一位自信、专一的人，对自己的职责了然于胸。只要能力允许，就一心一意想把自己的工作做好。现在的她时常迷失在两套不同的思路中。读书并非实干，这对她来说一直都是个问题。虽然女王年纪大了，但她依然是个实干家。

女王再次打开灯，拿起笔记本写道："不要将你的生活溶入你读的书。要在书里找到你的生活。"

然后她就睡着了。

···

之后的几个星期，人们注意到女王书读得少了。她总在沉思，甚至有时还会想得出神，有些心不在焉。但这些都与她读的书无关。女王不再去哪里都带本书。她桌上那一堆堆的书重新回到书架上，或是还给了图书馆，要不就是被收拾起来了。

不过，尽管读书少了，女王还是会长时间待在书房里，不时看看笔记本，偶尔写上一段。她明白自己的写作会比读书更不受欢迎。如果有人敲门，她会先把笔记本拂到抽屉里，然后才说："进来。"

女王发现，每当她写下点东西，即使只是笔记本里的一小段，她都感到十分高兴，就像以前读书的感觉一样。她再次意识到自己不想仅仅做个读者。读者和旁观者区别不大，而写作是一件需要实干的事，这正与她一直以来执行的职责相符。

与此同时，女王时常去图书馆，特别是温莎城堡的图书馆，翻阅自己以往的日志和无数参观访问的相册。这就是她自己过去所有的档案。

"陛下是想找点什么呢？"图书馆管理员问女王。他刚又给她搬来一堆材料。

"没什么，"女王回答，"我只是想回忆一下过去。究竟是哪一段过去我也说不准。"

"如果陛下记起来的话，请告诉我好了。最好是陛下自己写下来。女王陛下您就是一部活档案。"

女王觉得图书馆管理员用词可以更委婉一些，但他的意思还是明白的。她想，这不正有个人劝她写作吗。这样的话写作几乎就成了她的责任。女王一向认真负责，直到开始读书才有所懈怠。劝她写作与劝她发表作品是两件事。现在还没人劝她去发表自己的作品。

看到书从女王的桌子上渐渐消失，女王重又恢复了对职责的专注，凯文爵士和整个王室都十分高兴。女王还是不够准时，衣着风格也依然有些飘忽不定。她的女仆甚至会对她说："那件羊毛衫实在不能再穿了。"这些都是事实，但凯文爵士觉得，总体来说，除了这些一贯的不足之外，女王陛下已经不再痴迷于书籍，恢复了正常。

秋天的时候，女王在桑德林姆宫小住了几天，按计划访问了诺维奇市。她参加了教堂举行的一场弥撒，在步行街与行人进行了交谈，为一座新的消防站剪了彩，最后一项活动是大学里的午餐会。

女王的身旁是副校长和文学写作教授。她有点吃惊地发现，一只熟悉的瘦骨嶙峋的手从身后伸过来，将明虾头盘端给她。

"你好，诺曼。"她向他打招呼。

"女王陛下。"诺曼一边不卑不亢地回答，一边稳稳地将明虾头盘端给郡长。然后接着往下传菜。

"陛下认识希金斯啊？"文学写作教授问女王。

"过去认识。"女王说。她有点哀伤，因为诺曼似乎根本没有任何进步。看起来他似乎又回到了厨房。不过这一次不是她的厨房了。

副校长说："我们觉得，学生会很高兴能来做这次午餐的服务员。当然，我们会付他们工资的。对他们来说主要是一种难得的经历。"

文学写作教授说："希金斯非常有前途。他刚毕业，已经获得了不小的成功。"

女王有点恼怒。虽然她对诺曼热情地微笑，但他似乎打定主意不看她。上主菜面包牛肉卷的时候是这样，上甜点糖渍蜜梨佐冰淇淋时还是这样。她意识到诺曼可能是为了什么事在生她的闷气。她很少碰到这样的情况，只有小孩子和政府的一些部长偶尔会这样。臣民是没有权利对女王生闷气的。以前这样做是要被抓到伦敦塔里坐牢的。

几年前，女王是不会注意到诺曼举止的奇怪之处的。换了别人这样做，她也不会留意的。之所以女王现在会留意到这一点，那是因为她对人类情感的了解更加深入，而且能够进行换位思考。不过她还是不明白诺曼为什么会生她的气。

"书真是奇妙，是吧？"女王对副校长说。副校长连连称是。

女王接着说："虽然这让我听起来像把自己比做一块牛排，但我还是要说，书让我变得柔软了。"

副校长依然十分赞同。不过，他显然对女王要说什么毫无头绪。

女王转过头问教授："我在想，作为文学写作教授，你是否同意读书使人软弱，而写作恰恰相反呢？写作的人必须要坚强，是这样吗？"女王忽然和他讨论起专业话题，教授一时反应不过来。女王耐心等待着。"告诉我，"她想对教授说，"告诉我，我是对的。"就在这时，郡长起身准备恭送女王，所有的人也都跟着他站起来。女王心想，没人能回答她的问题。写作和读书一样，需要她自己去摸索。

虽然有些不合规矩，但午餐之后女王还是派人召唤了诺曼。现在女王的不准时已经是众所周知的了，在安排行程时已经考虑到了这点，所以她就花了半个小时了解了诺曼的大学生活，以及他当初是怎么会到东安格利亚大学来的。女王安排他第二天到桑德林姆宫来。她觉得既然诺曼已经有了写作经验，那正可以再次担任她的助手。

女王当天解雇了一个人。凯文爵士第二天早上进办公室的时候，发现自己的桌子已经被清理干净了。尽管安排诺曼上大学的决定对女王和诺曼都有利，但女王不喜欢有人骗她。真正的罪魁祸首是首相的特别顾问，凯文爵士却不得不替他背黑锅。凯文爵士本以为女王私人秘书的工作会让他进入政坛，结果却得到了一张回新西兰的机票和英联邦成员国大使的职位。这也算是进入了政坛，只不过路途远了点。

•••

不知不觉中，这一年女王八十岁了。这个生日引起了很大的关注，王室安排了各种各样的庆祝活动。有些活动女王喜欢，有些她并不喜欢。女王的顾问们一心想借此机会赢得那些总是反复无常的公众对君主制的热情。

因此，当女王决定召集所有曾担任过她智囊的人聚会的时候，人们也不觉得意外。其实这就是一次枢密院的聚会。枢密院的职位都是终身的，所以机构庞大，人数众多。枢密院很少一起开会，只有一些紧急关头才全体集会。不过，女王想，她一定要把这些人都请来喝一次隆重的下午茶。给他们多准备些茶点，包括火腿、牛舌、芥末、水芹、松饼和蛋糕，甚至还有酒浸果酱布丁。她觉得这样比一起吃晚餐更好，也更自在一些。

出席这次茶会的宾客都穿得比较随意，但女王还是像以往一样穿戴和仪容都无可挑剔。看着拥挤的人群，她心中感叹，居然有这么多人曾为自己出谋划策。由于人数众多，这次茶会安排在王宫最大的厅里。丰盛的茶

104

点放在两侧的小会客厅。女王高兴地漫步在人群中。她的身边并没有其他王室成员。不少王室成员也是枢密院的成员，但女王却没有邀请他们来参加这次茶会。她解释说："我见他们见得够多的了。不过我从来没有和你们这么多人一起见面。除非我去世，你们也不大可能聚在一起。一定要尝尝酒浸果酱布丁。好吃极了。"女王的心情从来没有这么好过。

来参加茶会的枢密院成员比预想的要多。对他们来说，与女王共进晚餐让人心烦，而一起喝下午茶则是件乐事。人来得实在太多，连椅子都不够了。侍从们不停地跑来跑去，为客人找坐的地方。这倒也成了茶会的一个乐趣。有人坐的是一般的镀金宴会椅，有人坐的是贵重的路易十五围手椅，还有人坐的是从前厅搬来印有王室字样的大靠背椅。一位卸任的大法官最后只能坐在一张洗手间里拿来的软木凳上。

女王平静地注视着这一切。她的椅子不是国王的御座，但比其他人的椅子要大上不少。女王一边端着茶喝，一边和人聊着天。直到所有人都舒服地坐下来之后，她才开始说话："过去这些年，我从你们那里得到了不少好建议，但我没有想到会有这么多。真是太多了！"

"陛下，也许我们应该一起唱'祝你生日快乐'！"坐在前排的首相说。

"别打岔，"女王说，"的确我已经八十岁了，今天也可以算是个生日聚会，但我还没决定要庆祝什么。至少可以这么说吧，我总算活到一个就是马上死了也不会让人吃惊的年纪了。"

人群发出一阵克制的笑声。女王自己也笑了。"我想，"她说，"你们喊上几句'不会，不会'，也许比较合适。"

有人照女王说的喊了几声。大家都志得意满地笑了。这个国家最显赫的女王和他们这些最杰出的人开玩笑，真是十分有趣。

"你们知道，我在位的时间很长。五十多年里，我经历了，注意不是送别了"——人群又是一阵笑声——"十位首相，六位坎特伯雷大主教，八位议长。还有，也许你们觉得这没有太多可比性——五十三条威尔士矮脚狗。正如布拉克内尔夫人所说的，真是风云变幻的一生啊！"

听众们发出会心的微笑，时不时还笑出声音来。这情景有点像是在小学的课堂上。

女王接着说："自然，生活还在继续。每一周都有令人关注的事发生，或是丑闻，或是掩盖丑闻，甚至是一场战争。今天是我的生日，你们可不能表现出一点不高兴的样子"——（首相在望着天花板，内政大臣则盯着地毯）——"我一直在思考未来的一切，从来都没有改变。到了八十岁，没有什么事是新鲜的，都是重复而已。"

"不过，你们有些人也知道，我一直都讨厌浪费。关于我的性格，有这样一个传说，说我在白金汉宫，走到哪里都要关灯。这个故事是想说明我比较小气，不过放在今天的社会背景中，可能正说明我对全球变暖的关注。既然我一向不喜欢浪费，那我自然也会这样对待自己一生的经历。这些经历不少是独一无二的，是我人生的精华。虽然我可能不过是个旁观者，但我的确对不少事情了解得更深入些。我的大多数经历"——女王轻轻点了点自己戴着帽子、一丝不乱的头——"都在这里。我不想浪费它们。问题是，怎么办呢？"

首相从椅子上站起身，正打算开口说话。

女王说："这个问题不需要回答。"

首相又坐了回去。

"你们有些人可能知道，过去几年我养成了读书的习惯。书以前所未有的方式丰富了我的生活，这是我没有想到的。不过，书能给我的有限。现在，我觉得，应该是我从一名读者成为，或者说尝试成为作者的时候了。"

首相又想站起来说话，这次女王和蔼地同意了。在她的记忆里，首相们对她说的话总是这样缺乏耐心。

"陛下，您可以写一本书。对，就是回忆您的童年，战争，对王宫的轰炸，还有您在空军妇女辅助队工作的事情。"

"是陆军运输勤务队。"女王纠正他。

"反正都是军队。"首相急急忙忙地接着说。"还有您的婚姻，以及您是如何戏剧性得知自己成了女王。这太吸引人了。"他得意地大笑。"这肯定会成为畅销书的。"

内政大臣也跟着说："肯定是本畅销全世界的书。"

"好——的。"女王说。"只不过，"她停了一下，"我并不想写一本这样的书。这种书谁都能写，而且已经有几个人写过了。在我看来，他们写得全都乏味至极。我想写的是另外一种类型的书。"

首相的情绪并没有受到打击。他礼貌地抬起头，显示出有兴趣的样子。也许老太太是想写本游记。那也会畅销的。

女王镇静了一下，说道："我想写的书更激进，更有……挑战性。"

"激进"和"挑战性"这两个词都是首相常说的。他依然保持平静。

"你们有人读过普鲁斯特吗？"女王问道。

有些耳朵不好的人低声询问普鲁斯特是谁。有些读过的人举起了手。看到首相没有举手，内阁里一位读过普鲁斯特的年轻成员也放弃了举手的念头。他觉得那样做对他肯定没好处。

女王数了数举起来的手。"八，九，十——"她注意到，这些人大多数都是以前的内阁成员。"噢，这有点意思。不过我一点也不意外。如果是麦克米兰先生的内阁的话，包括他自己在内，肯定十二个人都读过。这么说有点不公平，我自己那时也没读过普鲁斯特。"

"我读过特罗洛普。"一位前外交部长说。

"这很好，"女王回答，"不过特罗洛普不是普鲁斯特。"内政大臣这两个作者的书都没读过，但他还是道貌岸然地跟着女王的话直点头。

"普鲁斯特的书很长，如果你们夏天不去滑水的话，也许有时间读完它。在小说的结尾，叙述者马塞尔回顾自己平淡的一生，决心写一本小说记录它。这正是我们刚刚读完的这本小说。它为我们揭开了不少记忆与回忆的秘密。"

"尽管我的人生与马塞尔不同，取得了不少成就，但我仍然觉得自己需要通过分析和反思来让它焕发光彩。"

"分析？"首相问道。

"还有反思。"女王回答。

内政大臣忽然想到一个在下议院会很受欢迎的笑话，便大着胆子说了出来："我们是否可以这样说，陛下写书的决定是来自您读的一本书，而且还是一本法国书？呵呵。"

人群中有一两声低低的笑声。女王却根本没有觉得这是个笑话。事实上这个笑话的确很冷。"不对，内政大臣。你肯定知道，书不会促使人行动，但它们会支持你无意识中已经决定的事情。你在书中确认自己的信念。作为一本书，它的作用不会超出书的世界。"

有些早已卸任的官员听出来现在的女王与他们过去认识的女王完全不同，不禁对她说的话入了迷。但大多数人都在沉默中如坐针毡，一点也不知道女王究竟想说什么。女王明白这一点。她泰然自若地接着说："你们对我说的话有点迷惑不解，但我可以肯定地说，你们其实早已了解这个道理。"

情形好像又回到了学校里老师和学生的对话。"在每一次公众质询之前，隐含的前提不就是寻求证据来支持你们早已做好的决定吗？"

最年轻的部长笑出声来，然后立刻就后悔了。因为首相没有笑。如果女王以这样的语气来写书的话，那她要写什么实在让人难以琢磨。"陛下，我还是认为您最好就写写您的生活经历。"他勉强地说。

"那不行。我对简单的回忆不感兴趣。我希望我写的书思虑更为完备。我说的思虑完备可不是要体谅他人，"女王说，"这句话是个玩笑。"

没人大笑。首相的微笑已经变了形，龇牙咧嘴，十

111

分可怕。

"谁知道呢，"女王开心地说，"说不定会写成一本文学书。"

"我认为，"首相说道，"陛下是凌驾于文学之上的。"

"凌驾于文学之上？"女王问道。"谁能凌驾于文学之上呢？那你也可以说我是凌驾于人类之上了。不过，就像我说的，我的目的主要并不在于文学，而是分析与反思。这十个首相究竟怎么样？"她愉快地笑着说。"有太多可以思考的了。我看到这个国家多次陷入战争，简直不愿意回忆那些不愉快的经历。这也同样值得思考。"

女王依然微笑着。不过只有那些最老的官员跟着她一起笑。其他的人都显得忧心忡忡。

"我曾接见并招待过不少来访的国家元首。其中有些人是可怕的骗子和无赖。他们的妻子也好不到哪去。"这句话总算有了反应。一些人悔恨地直点头。

"我戴着雪白的手套和那些沾满鲜血的手握手，客气礼貌地与那些屠杀孩童的人交谈。我在粪便和淤血里跋涉。我时常想，作为女王，最基本的装备就是一双高帮靴。"

"人们经常说我非常具有判断力，但这只不过是委婉地说我不具备其他的能力。也许正因为这样，在我经历的各届政府中，我都不得不被动地参与一些不明智的决议。这些决议不少都令我感到耻辱。有时候，我觉得自己就像一只香味蜡烛，被用来给政权和政策增加香味。君主制现在不过是政府问题的除臭剂。"

"我是英国女王，英联邦的元首。但是，在过去的五十年里，很多时候我并没有为此骄傲，反而觉得羞耻。不过，"女王站了起来，"我们还是要分清楚主次。毕竟今天是一次聚会。所以，我们还是先喝点香槟，然后接着再说。"

香槟很好。可是，首相在侍者中看见了诺曼的身影，立刻就没了胃口。他偷偷沿着走廊溜到厕所，给司法部长打了个电话。司法部长尽力安慰了首相。得到一些法律指导之后，首相立刻告诉了全体内阁成员。所以当女王回来的时候，房间里的气氛轻松了许多。

"我们一直在讨论您说的话。"首相先说。

"别着急，"女王回答，"我还没说完呢。你们千万不要以为我要写的——其实我已经开始写了——是那种无聊小报最喜欢的低级的、王宫生活隐私之类的垃圾。不是那种东西。我从没写过书。我希望我的书"——她停顿了一下——"能超越它的时代背景，自成一格，是一部与现实时代不相关的历史，和我的生活以及政治基本是毫不相干的。这样你们也许会放心些吧。我想在写作中讨论书与人，而不是写些流言蜚语。我从不喜欢那些。我也不会直截了当地写。我记得是 E. M. 福斯特说过的：'要写出全部的真实，但不需要写得直白，可以用曲笔。'是他说的吗？"女王问在座的宾客。"还是艾米莉·狄金森？"

不出意料，没人回答女王的问题。

"我不能再多谈了，否则这本书永远也写不出来。"

想到很多人宣称要写书，但一直也没写出来，首相并没感到安慰。女王的责任感和个性保证了她肯定会写出这本书的。

女王高兴地问首相："好了，你刚才在说什么？"

首相站起身来说："陛下，我们尊重您的计划。"——他的语气轻松而友善——"但我觉得还是应该提醒您，您的地位十分特殊。"

"我从未忘记这一点，"女王回答，"继续说。"

"国王从没出版过书。这应该没错吧。"

女王对他摇了摇手。她记得这是诺埃尔·科沃德[1]爱用的手势。"首相，你说得并不准确。比如我的祖先亨利八世就写过反对异教的书。所以我今天还有着信仰捍卫者的头衔。与我同名的伊丽莎白一世也写过。"

首相正想反驳。

"别急。我知道那有所不同。但我的老祖母维多利亚女王也写过书——《高地日志》。那是一本很沉闷的书，说让人难以卒读一点也不过分。我不会以此为榜样的。当然，"——女王注视着她的第一位首相——"还有我的叔叔温莎公爵。他写过《国王的故事》，记述了他的婚姻和后来的冒险经历。别的不说，这无疑可以算是先例了吧？"

司法部长的建议正好可以用上了。首相带着歉意微笑着反驳说："陛下，我同意您的说法。不过，殿下当

1　诺埃尔·科沃德爵士（Sir Noël Coward，1899—1973），英国剧作家、作曲家、导演、演员和歌手，以其机智和浮夸风格闻名。

年是以温莎公爵的身份写的书。他之所以能写书是因为他已经退位了。"

"噢，我还没说吗？"女王问道。"不过……你们觉得我为什么会把你们都请来呢？"

THE UNCOMMON READER

—— Alan Bennett ——

AT WINDSOR it was the evening of the state banquet and as the president of France took his place beside Her Majesty, the royal family formed up behind and the procession slowly moved off and through into the Waterloo Chamber.

'Now that I have you to myself,' said the Queen, smiling to left and right as they glided through the glittering throng, 'I've been longing to ask you about the writer Jean Genet.'

'Ah,' said the president. 'Oui.'

The 'Marseillaise' and the national anthem made for a pause in the proceedings, but when they had taken their seats Her Majesty turned to the president and resumed.

'Homosexual and jailbird, was he nevertheless as bad as he was painted? Or, more to the point' – and she took up her soup spoon – 'was he as good?'

Unbriefed on the subject of the glabrous playwright and novelist, the president looked wildly about for his minister of culture. But she was being addressed by the Archbishop of Canterbury.

'Jean Genet,' said the Queen again, helpfully. 'Vous le connaissez?'

'Bien sûr,' said the president.

'Il m'intéresse,' said the Queen.

'Vraiment?' The president put down his spoon. It was going to be a long evening.

IT WAS the dogs' fault. They were snobs and ordinarily, having been in the garden, would have gone up the front steps, where a footman generally opened them the door. Today, though, for some reason they careered along the terrace, barking their heads off, and scampered down the steps again and round the end along the side of the house, where she could hear them yapping at something in one of the yards.

It was the City of Westminster travelling library, a large removal-like van parked next to the bins outside one of the kitchen doors. This wasn't a part of the palace she saw much of, and she had certainly never seen the library there before, nor presumably had the dogs, hence the din, so having failed in her attempt to calm them down she went up the little steps of the van in order to apologise.

The driver was sitting with his back to her, sticking a label on a book, the only seeming borrower a thin ginger-haired boy in white overalls crouched in the aisle reading. Neither of them took any notice of the new arrival, so she coughed and said, 'I'm sorry about this awful racket,' whereupon the driver got up so suddenly he banged his head on the Reference section and the boy in the aisle scrambled to his feet and upset Photography & Fashion.

She put her head out of the door. 'Shut up this minute, you silly creatures' – which, as had been the move's intention, gave the driver/librarian time to compose himself and the boy to pick up the books.

'One has never seen you here before, Mr...'

'Hutchings, Your Majesty. Every Wednesday, ma'am.'

'Really? I never knew that. Have you come far?'

'Only from Westminster, ma'am.'

'And you are ... ?'

'Norman, ma'am. Seakins.'

'And where do you work?'

'In the kitchen, ma'am.'

'Oh. Do you have much time for reading?'

'Not really, ma'am.'

'I'm the same. Though now that one is here I suppose one ought to borrow a book.'

Mr Hutchings smiled helpfully.

'Is there anything you would recommend?'

'What does Your Majesty like?'

The Queen hesitated, because to tell the truth she wasn't sure. She'd never taken much interest in reading. She read, of course, as one did, but liking books was something she left to other people. It was a hobby and it was in the nature of her job that she didn't have hobbies. Jogging, growing roses, chess or rock-climbing, cake decoration, model aeroplanes. No. Hobbies involved preferences and preferences had to be avoided; preferences excluded people. One had no preferences. Her job was to take an interest, not to be interested herself. And besides, reading wasn't doing. She was a doer. So she gazed round the book-lined van and played for time. 'Is one allowed to borrow a book? One doesn't have a ticket?'

'No problem,' said Mr Hutchings.

'One is a pensioner,' said the Queen, not that she was

sure that made any difference.

'Ma'am can borrow up to six books.'

'Six? Heavens!'

Meanwhile the ginger-haired young man had made his choice and given his book to the librarian to stamp. Still playing for time, the Queen picked it up.

'What have you chosen, Mr Seakins?' expecting it to be, well, she wasn't sure what she expected, but it wasn't what it was. 'Oh. Cecil Beaton. Did you know him?'

'No, ma'am.'

'No, of course not. You'd be too young. He always used to be round here, snapping away. And a bit of a tartar. Stand here, stand there. Snap, snap. So there's a book about him now?'

'Several, ma'am.'

'Really? I suppose everyone gets written about sooner or later.'

She riffled through it. 'There's probably a picture of me in it somewhere. Oh yes. That one. Of course, he wasn't just a photographer. He designed, too. *Oklahoma*, things like that.'

'I think it was *My Fair Lady*, ma'am.'

'Oh, was it?' said the Queen, unused to being contradicted.

'Where did you say you worked?' She put the book back in the boy's big red hands.

'In the kitchens, ma'am.'

She had still not solved her problem, knowing that if she left without a book it would seem to Mr Hutchings that the library was somehow lacking. Then on a shelf of rather worn-looking volumes she saw a name she remembered. 'Ivy Compton-Burnett! I can read that.' She took the book out and gave it to Mr Hutchings to stamp.

'What a treat!' She hugged it unconvincingly before opening it. 'Oh. The last time it was taken out was in 1989.'

'She's not a popular author, ma'am.'

'Why, I wonder? I made her a dame.'

Mr Hutchings refrained from saying that this wasn't necessarily the road to the public's heart.

The Queen looked at the photograph on the back of the jacket. 'Yes. I remember that hair, a roll like a pie-crust that went right round her head.' She smiled and Mr Hutchings knew that the visit was over. 'Goodbye.'

He inclined his head as they had told him at the library to do should this eventuality ever arise, and the Queen went off in the direction of the garden with the dogs madly barking again, while Norman, bearing his Cecil Beaton, skirted a chef lounging by the bins having a cigarette and went back to the kitchens.

Shutting up the van and driving away, Mr Hutchings reflected that a novel by Ivy Compton-Burnett would take some reading. He had never got very far with her himself and thought, rightly, that borrowing the book had just been a polite gesture. Still, it was one that he appreciated and as more than a courtesy. The council was always threatening to cut back on the library and the patronage of so distinguished a borrower (or customer as the council preferred to call it) would do him no harm.

'We have a travelling library,' The Queen said to her husband that evening. 'Comes every Wednesday.'

'Jolly good. Wonders never cease.'

'You remember *Oklahoma*?'

'Yes. We saw it when we were engaged.' Extraordinary to think of it, the dashing blond boy he had been.

'Was that Cecil Beaton?' said the Queen.

'No idea. Never liked the fellow. Green shoes.'

'Smelled delicious.'

'What's that?'

'A book. I borrowed it.'

'Dead, I suppose.'

'Who?'

'The Beaton fellow.'

'Oh yes. Everybody's dead.'

'Good show, though.'

And he went off to bed glumly singing 'Oh, what a beautiful morning' as the Queen opened her book.

THE FOLLOWING week she had intended to give the book to a lady-in-waiting to return, but finding herself taken captive by her private secretary and forced to go through the diary in far greater detail than she thought necessary, she was able to cut off discussion of a tour round a road-research laboratory by suddenly declaring that it was Wednesday and she had to go to change her book at the travelling library. Her private secretary, Sir Kevin Scatchard, an over-conscientious New Zealander of whom great things were expected, was left to gather up his papers and wonder why ma'am needed a travelling library when she had several of the stationary kind of her own.

Minus the dogs this visit was somewhat calmer, though once again Norman was the only borrower.

'How did you find it, ma'am?' asked Mr Hutchings.

'Dame Ivy? A little dry. And everybody talks the same way, did you notice that?'

'To tell you the truth, ma'am, I never got through more than a few pages. How far did Your Majesty get?'

'Oh, to the end. Once I start a book I finish it. That was the way one was brought up. Books, bread and butter, mashed potato – one finishes what's on one's plate. That's always been my philosophy.'

'There was actually no need to have brought the book back, ma'am. We're downsizing and all the books on that shelf are free.'

'You mean, I can have it?' She clutched the book to her. 'I'm glad I came. Good afternoon, Mr Seakins. More Cecil Beaton?'

Norman showed her the book he was looking at, this time something on David Hockney. She leafed through it, gazing unperturbed at young men's bottoms hauled out of Californian swimming-pools or lying together on unmade beds.

'Some of them,' she said, 'some of them don't seem altogether finished. This one is quite definitely smudged.'

'I think that was his style then, ma'am,' said Norman.

'He's actually quite a good draughtsman.'

The Queen looked at Norman again. 'You work in the kitchens?'

'Yes, ma'am.'

She hadn't really intended to take out another book, but decided that now she was here it was perhaps easier to do it than not, though, regarding what book to choose, she felt as baffled as she had done the previous week. The truth was she didn't really want a book at all and certainly not another Ivy Compton-Burnett, which was too hard going altogether. So it was lucky that this time her eye happened to fall on a reissued volume of Nancy Mitford's *The Pursuit of Love*. She picked it up. 'Now. Didn't her sister marry the Mosley man?'

Mr Hutchings said he believed she did.

'And the mother-in-law of another sister was my mistress of the robes?'

'I don't know about that, ma'am.'

'Then of course there was the rather sad sister who had the fling with Hitler. And one became a Communist. And I think there was another besides. But this is Nancy?'

'Yes, ma'am.'

'Good.'

Novels seldom came as well connected as this and the Queen felt correspondingly reassured, so it was with some confidence that she gave the book to Mr Hutchings to be stamped.

The Pursuit of Love turned out to be a fortunate choice and in its way a momentous one. Had Her Majesty gone for another duff read, an early George Eliot, say, or a late Henry James, novice reader that she was she might have been put off reading for good and there would be no story to tell. Books, she would have thought, were work.

As it was, with this one she soon became engrossed and, passing her bedroom that night clutching his hot-water bottle, the duke heard her laugh out loud. He put his head round the door. 'All right, old girl?'

'Of course. I'm reading.'

'Again?' And he went off, shaking his head.

The next morning she had a little sniffle and, having no engagements, stayed in bed saying she felt she might be getting flu. This was uncharacteristic and also not true; it was actually so that she could get on with her book.

'The Queen has a slight cold' was what the nation was told, but what it was not told, and what the Queen herself did not know, was that this was only the first of a series of accommodations, some of them far-reaching, that her reading was going to involve.

The following day the Queen had one of her regular sessions with her private secretary, with as one of the items on the agenda what these days is called human resources.

'In my day,' she had told him, 'it was called personnel.' Although actually it wasn't. It was called 'the servants'. She mentioned this, too, knowing it would provoke a reaction.

'That could be misconstrued, ma'am,' said Sir Kevin. 'One's aim is always to give the public no cause for offence. "Servants" sends the wrong message.'

'Human resources,' said the Queen, 'sends no message at all. At least not to me. However, since we're on the subject of human resources, there is one human resource currently working in the kitchens whom I would like promoted, or at any rate brought upstairs.'

Sir Kevin had never heard of Seakins but on consulting several underlings Norman was eventually located.

'I cannot understand,' said Her Majesty, 'what he is doing in the kitchen in the first place. He's obviously a young man of some intelligence.'

'Not dolly enough,' said the equerry, though to the private secretary not to the Queen. 'Thin, ginger-haired. Have a heart.'

'Madam seems to like him,' said Sir Kevin. 'She wants him on her floor.'

Thus it was that Norman found himself emancipated from washing dishes and fitted (with some difficulty) into a page's uniform and brought into waiting, where one of his first jobs was predictably to do with the library.

Not free the following Wednesday (gymnastics in Nuneaton), the Queen gave Norman her Nancy Mitford to return, telling him that there was apparently a sequel and she wanted to read that too, plus anything else besides he thought she might fancy.

This commission caused him some anxiety. Well read up to a point, he was largely self-taught, his reading tending to be determined by whether an author was gay or not. Fairly wide remit though this was, it did narrow things down a bit, particularly when choosing a book for someone else, and the more so when that someone else happened to be the Queen.

Nor was Mr Hutchings much help, except that when

he mentioned dogs as a subject that might interest Her Majesty it reminded Norman of something he had read that could fit the bill, J. R. Ackerley's novel *My Dog Tulip*. Mr Hutchings was dubious, pointing out that it was a gay book.

'Is it?' said Norman innocently. 'I didn't realise that. She'll think it's just about the dog.'

He took the books up to the Queen's floor and, having been told to make himself as scarce as possible, when the duke came by hid behind a boulle cabinet.

'Saw this extraordinary creature this afternoon,' HRH reported later. 'Ginger-stick-in-waiting.'

'That would be Norman,' said the Queen. 'I met him in the travelling library. He used to work in the kitchen.'

'I can see why,' said the duke.

'He's very intelligent,' said the Queen.

'He'll have to be,' said the duke. 'Looking like that.'

'Tulip,' said the Queen to Norman later. 'Funny name for a dog.'

'It's supposed to be fiction, ma'am, only the author did have a dog in life, an Alsatian.' (He didn't tell her its name was Queenie.) 'So it's really disguised auto-biography.'

'Oh,' said the Queen. 'Why disguise it?'

Norman thought she would find out when she read the book, but he didn't say so.

'None of his friends liked the dog, ma'am.'

'One knows that feeling very well, 'said the Queen, and Norman nodded solemnly, the royal dogs being generally unpopular. The Queen smiled. What a find Norman was. She knew that she inhibited, made people shy, and few of the servants behaved like themselves. Oddity though he was, Norman was himself and seemed incapable of being anything else. That was very rare.

The Queen, though, might have been less pleased had she known that Norman was unaffected by her because she seemed to him so ancient, her royalty obliterated by her seniority. Queen she might be but she was also an old lady, and since Norman's introduction to the world of work had been via an old people's home on Tyneside old ladies held no terrors for him. To Norman she was his employer, but her age made her as much patient as Queen and in both capacities to be humoured, though this was, it's true, before he woke up to how sharp she was and how much wasted.

She was also intensely conventional and when she had started to read she thought perhaps she ought to do some of it at least in the place set aside for the purpose, namely the palace library. But though it was called the library and was indeed lined with books, a book was seldom if ever read there. Ultimatums were delivered here, lines drawn, prayer books compiled and marriages decided upon, but should one want to curl up with a book the library was not the place. It was not easy even to lay hands on something to read, as on the open shelves, so called, the books were sequestered behind locked and gilded grilles. Many of them were priceless, which was another discouragement. No, if reading was to be done it were better done in a place not set aside for it. The Queen thought that there might be a lesson there and she went back upstairs.

Having finished the Nancy Mitford sequel, *Love in a Cold Climate*, the Queen was delighted to see she had written others, and though some of them seemed to be history she put them on her (newly started) reading list, which she kept in her desk. Meanwhile she got on with Norman's choice, *My Dog Tulip* by J. R. Ackerley. (Had she met him? She thought not.) She enjoyed the book if only because, as Norman had said, the dog in question seemed even more of a handful than hers and just about as unpopular. Seeing that Ackerley had written an autobiography, she sent Norman down to the London Library to borrow it. Patron of the London Library, she had seldom set foot in it and neither, of course, had Norman, but he came back full of wonder and excitement at how old-fashioned it was, saying it was the sort of library he had only read about in books and had thought confined to the past. He had wandered through its labyrinthine stacks marvelling that these were all books that he (or rather She) could borrow at will. So infectious was his enthusiasm that next time, the Queen thought, she might accompany him.

She read Ackerley's account of himself, unsurprised to find that, being a homosexual, he had worked for the BBC, though feeling also that he had had a sad life. His dog intrigued her, though she was disconcerted by the almost veterinary intimacies with which he indulged the creature. She was also surprised that the Guards seemed to be as readily available as the book made out and at such a reasonable tariff. She would have liked to have known more about this; but though she had equerries who were in the Guards she hardly felt able to ask.

E. M. Forster figured in the book, with whom she remembered spending an awkward half-hour when she invested him with the CH. Mouse-like and shy, he had said little and in such a small voice she had found him almost impossible to communicate with. Still, he was a bit of a dark horse. Sitting there with his hands pressed together like something out of *Alice in Wonderland*, he gave no hint of what he was thinking, and so she was pleasantly surprised to find on reading his biography that he had said afterwards that had she been a boy he would have fallen in love with her.

Of course he couldn't actually have said this to her face, she realised that, but the more she read the more she regretted how she intimidated people and wished that writers in particular had the courage to say what they later wrote down. What she was finding also was how one book led to another, doors kept opening wherever she turned and the days weren't long enough for the reading she wanted to do.

But there was regret, too, and mortification at the many opportunities she had missed. As a child she had met Masefield and Walter de la Mare; nothing much she could have said to them, but she had met T. S. Eliot, too, and there was Priestley and Philip Larkin and even Ted Hughes, to whom she'd taken a bit of a shine but who remained nonplussed in her presence. And it was because she had at that time read so little of what they had written that she could not find anything to say and they, of course, had not said much of interest to her. What a waste.

She made the mistake of mentioning this to Sir Kevin.

'But ma'am must have been briefed, surely?'

'Of course,' said the Queen, 'but briefing is not reading. In fact it is the antithesis of reading. Briefing is terse, factual and to the point. Reading is untidy, discursive and perpetually inviting. Briefing closes down a subject, reading opens it up.'

'I wonder whether I can bring Your Majesty back to the visit to the shoe factory,' said Sir Kevin.

'Next time,' said the Queen shortly. 'Where did I put my book?'

HAVING DISCOVERED the delights of reading herself, Her Majesty was keen to pass them on.

'Do you read, Summers?' she said to the chauffeur en route for Northampton.

'Read, ma'am?'

'Books?'

'When I get the chance, ma'am. I never seem to find

the time.'

'That's what a lot of people say. One must make the time. Take this morning. You're going to be sitting outside the town hall waiting for me. You could read then.'

'I have to watch the motor, ma'am. This is the Midlands. Vandalism is universal.'

With Her Majesty safely delivered into the hands of the lord lieutenant, Summers did a precautionary circuit of the motor, then settled down in his seat. Read? Of course he read. Everybody read. He opened the glove compartment and took out his copy of the *Sun*.

Others, notably Norman, were more sympathetic, and from him she made no attempt to hide her shortcomings as a reader or her lack of cultural credentials altogether.

'Do you know,' she said one afternoon as they were reading in her study, 'do you know the area in which one would truly excel?'

'No, ma'am?'

'The pub quiz. One has been everywhere, seen everything and though one might have difficulty with pop music and some sport, when it comes to the capital of Zimbabwe, say, or the principal exports of New

South Wales, I have all that at my fingertips.'

'And I could do the pop,' said Norman.

'Yes,' said the Queen. 'We would make a good team. Ah well. The road not travelled. Who's that?'

'Who, ma'am?'

'The road not travelled. Look it up.'

Norman looked it up in the *Dictionary of Quotations* to find that it was Robert Frost.

'I know the word for you,' said the Queen.

'Ma'am?'

'You run errands, you change my library books, you look up awkward words in the dictionary and find me quotations. Do you know what you are?'

'I used to be a skivvy, ma'am.'

'Well, you're not a skivvy now. You're my amanuensis.'

Norman looked it up in the dictionary the Queen now kept always on her desk. 'One who writes from dictation, copies manuscripts. A literary assistant.'

The new amanuensis had a chair in the corridor, handy for the Queen's office, on which, when he was not on call or running errands, he would spend his time reading. This did him no good at all with the other pages, who thought he was on a cushy number and not comely enough to deserve it. Occasionally a passing equerry would stop and ask him if he had nothing better to do than read, and to begin with he had been stuck for a reply. Nowadays, though, he said he was reading something for Her Majesty, which was often true but was also satisfactorily irritating and so sent the equerry away in a bad temper.

READING MORE and more, the Queen now drew her books from various libraries, including some of her own, but for sentimental reasons and because she liked Mr Hutchings, she still occasionally made a trip down to the kitchen yard to patronise the travelling library.

One Wednesday afternoon, though, it wasn't there, nor the following week either. Norman was straight away on the case, only to be told that the visit to the palace had been cancelled due to all-round cutbacks. Undeterred, Norman eventually tracked the library down to Pimlico, where in a schoolyard he found Mr Hutchings still doggedly at the wheel, sticking labels on the books. Mr Hutchings told him that though he had pointed out to the Libraries Outreach Department that Her Majesty was one of their borrowers this cut no ice with the council, which, prior to axing the visits, said that inquiries had been made at the palace and it had disclaimed any interest in the matter.

Told this by the outraged Norman, the Queen seemed unsurprised, but though she said nothing to him it confirmed what she had suspected, namely that in royal circles reading, or at any rate her reading, was not well looked on.

Small setback though the loss of the travelling library was, there was one happy outcome, as Mr Hutchings found himself figuring on the next honours list; it was, admittedly, in quite a lowly capacity, but numbered among those who had done Her Majesty some special and personal service. This was not well looked on either, particularly by Sir Kevin.

Since he was from New Zealand and something of a departure when he was appointed, Sir Kevin Scatchard had inevitably been hailed in the press as a new broom, a young(ish) man who would sweep away some of the redundant deference and more flagrant flummeries that were monarchy's customary accretions, the Crown in this version pictured as not unlike Miss Havisham's wedding feast – the cobwebbed chandeliers, the mice-infested cake and Sir Kevin as Mr Pip tearing down the rotting curtains to let in the light. The Queen, who had the advantage of having once been a breath of fresh air herself, was unconvinced by this scenario, suspecting that this brisk Antipodean wind would in due course blow itself out. Private secretaries, like prime ministers, came and went, and in Sir Kevin's case the Queen felt she might simply be a stepping stone to those corporate heights for which he was undoubtedly headed. He was a graduate of the Harvard Business School and one of his publicly stated aims ('setting out our stall', as he put it) was to make the monarchy more accessible. The opening of Buckingham Palace to visitors had been a step down this road, as was the use of the garden for occasional concerts, pop and otherwise. The reading, though, made him uneasy.

'I feel, ma'am, that while not exactly elitist it sends the wrong message. It tends to exclude.'

'Exclude? Surely most people can read?'

'They can read, ma'am, but I'm not sure that they do.'

'Then, Sir Kevin, I am setting them a good example.'

She smiled sweetly, while noting that these days Sir Kevin was much less of a New Zealander than when he had first been appointed, his accent now with only a tincture of that Kiwi connection about which Her Majesty knew he was sensitive and of which he did not wish to be reminded (Norman had told her).

Another delicate issue was his name. The private secretary felt burdened by his name: Kevin was not the name he would have chosen for himself and disliking it made him more aware of the number of times the Queen used it, though she could hardly have been aware of how demeaning he felt it.

In fact she knew perfectly well (Norman again), but to her everybody's name was immaterial, as indeed was everything else, their clothes, their voice, their class. She was a genuine democrat, perhaps the only one in the country.

To Sir Kevin, though, it seemed that she used his name unnecessarily often, and there were times when he was sure she gave it a breath of New Zealand, that land of sheep and Sunday afternoons, and a country which, as head of the Commonwealth, she had several times visited and claimed to be enthusiastic about.

'It's important,' said Sir Kevin, 'that Your Majesty should stay focused.'

'When you say "stay focused", Sir Kevin, I suppose you mean one should keep one's eye on the ball. Well, I've had my eye on ball for more than fifty years so I think these days one is allowed the occasional glance to the boundary.' She felt that her metaphor had probably slipped a little there, not, though, that Sir Kevin noticed.

'I can understand,' he said, 'Your Majesty's need to pass the time.'

'Pass the time?' said the Queen. 'Books are not about passing the time. They're about other lives. Other worlds. Far from wanting time to pass, Sir Kevin, one just wishes one had more of it. If one wanted to pass the time one could go to New Zealand.'

With two mentions of his name and one of New Zealand Sir Kevin retired hurt. Still, he had made a point and he would have been gratified to know that it left the Queen troubled, and wondering why it was that at this particular time in her life she had suddenly felt the pull of books. Where had this appetite come from?

Few people, after all, had seen more of the world than she had. There was scarcely a country she had not visited, a notability she had not met. Herself part of the panoply of the world, why now was she intrigued by books which, whatever else they might be, were just a reflection of the world or a version of it? Books? She had seen the real thing.

'I read, I think,' she said to Norman, 'because one

has a duty to find out what people are like,' a trite enough remark of which Norman took not much notice, feeling himself under no such obligation and reading purely for pleasure, not enlightenment, though part of the pleasure was the enlightenment, he could see that. But duty did not come into it.

To someone with the background of the Queen, though, pleasure had always taken second place to duty. If she could feel she had a duty to read then she could set about it with a clear conscience, with the pleasure, if pleasure there was, incidental. But why did it take possession of her now? This she did not discuss with Norman, as she felt it had to do with who she was and the position she occupied.

The appeal of reading, she thought, lay in its indifference: there was something lofty about literature. Books did not care who was reading them or whether one read them or not. All readers were equal, herself included. Literature, she thought, is a commonwealth; letters a republic. Actually she had heard this phrase, the republic of letters, used before, at graduation ceremonies, honorary degrees and the like, though without knowing quite what it meant. At that time talk of a republic of any sort she had thought mildly insulting and in her actual presence tactless to say the least. It was only now she understood what it meant. Books did not defer. All readers were equal, and this took her back to the beginning of her life. As a girl, one of her greatest thrills had been on VE night, when she and her sister had slipped out of the gates and mingled unrecognised with the crowds. There was something of that, she felt, to reading. It was anonymous; it was shared; it was common. And she who had led a life apart now found that she craved it. Here in these pages and between these covers she could go unrecognised.

These doubts and self-questionings, though, were just the beginning. Once she got into her stride it ceased to seem strange to her that she wanted to read, and books, to which she had taken so cautiously, gradually came to be her element.

ONE OF THE Queen's recurrent royal responsibilities was to open Parliament, an obligation she had never previously found particularly burdensome and actually rather enjoyed: to be driven down the Mall on a bright autumn morning even after fifty years was something of a treat. But not any more. She was dreading the two hours the whole thing was due to take, though fortunately they were in the coach, not the open carriage, so she could take along her book. She'd got quite good at reading and waving, the trick being to keep the book below the level of the window and to keep focused on it and not on the crowds. The duke didn't like it one bit, of course, but goodness it helped.

Which was all very well, except it was only when she was actually in the coach, with the procession drawn up in the palace forecourt and ready for the off, that, as she put on her glasses, she realised she'd forgotten the book. And while the duke fumes in the corner and the postillions fidget, the horses shift and the harness clinks, Norman is rung on the mobile. The Guardsmen stand at ease and the procession waits. The officer in charge looks at his watch. Two minutes late. Knowing nothing displeases Her Majesty more and knowing nothing of the book, he does not look forward to the repercussions that must inevitably follow. But here is Norman, skittering across the gravel with the book thoughtfully hidden in a shawl, and off they go.

Still, it is an ill-tempered royal couple that is driven down the Mall, the duke waving viciously from his side, the Queen listlessly from hers, and at some speed, too, as the procession tries to pick up the two minutes that have been lost.

At Westminster she popped the offending book behind a cushion in the carriage ready for the journey back, mindful as she sat on the throne and embarked on her speech of how tedious was the twaddle she was called on to deliver and that this was actually the only occasion when she got to read aloud to the nation. 'My government will do this...my government will do that.' It was so barbarously phrased and wholly devoid of style or interest that she felt it demeaned the very act of reading itself, with this year's performance even more garbled than usual as she, too, tried to pick up the missing couple of minutes.

It was with some relief that she got back into the coach and reached behind the cushion for her book. It was not there. Steadfastly waving as they rumbled along, she surreptitiously felt behind the other cushions.

'You're not sitting on it?'

'Sitting on what?'

'My book.'

'No, I am not. Some British Legion people here, and wheelchairs. Wave, for God's sake.'

When they arrived at the palace she had a word with

Grant, the young footman in charge, who said that while ma'am had been in the Lords the sniffer dogs had been round and security had confiscated the book. He thought it had probably been exploded.

'Exploded?' said the Queen. 'But it was Anita Brookner.'

The young man, who seemed remarkably undeferential, said security may have thought it was a device.

The Queen said: 'Yes. That is exactly what it is. A book is a device to ignite the imagination.'

The footman said: 'Yes, ma'am.'

It was as if he was talking to his grandmother, and not for the first time the Queen was made unpleasantly aware of the hostility her reading seemed to arouse.

'Very well,' she said. 'Then you should inform security that I shall expect to find another copy of the same book, vetted and explosive-free, waiting on my desk tomorrow morning. And another thing. The carriage cushions are filthy. Look at my gloves.' Her Majesty departed.

'Fuck,' said the footman, fishing out the book from where he had been told to hide it down the front of his breeches. But of the lateness of the procession, to everyone's surprise nothing was officially said.

149

This dislike of the Queen's reading was not confined to the household. Whereas in the past walkies had meant a noisy and unrestrained romp in the grounds, these days, once she was out of sight of the house Her Majesty sank onto the nearest seat and took out her book. Occasionally she threw a bored biscuit in the direction of the dogs, but there was none of that ball-throwing, stick-fetching and orchestrated frenzy that used to enliven their perambulations. Indulged and bad-tempered though they were, the dogs were not unintelligent, so it was not surprising that in a short space of time they came to hate books as the spoilsports they were (and always have been).

Did Her Majesty ever let a book fall to the carpet it would straightaway be leaped on by any attendant dog, worried and slavered over and borne to the distant reaches of the palace or wherever so that it could be satisfyingly torn apart. The James Tait Black prize notwithstanding, Ian McEwan had ended up like this and even A. S. Byatt. Patron of the London Library though she was, Her Majesty regularly found herself on the phone apologising to the renewals clerk for the loss of yet another volume.

The dogs disliked Norman, too, and in so far as

the young man could be blamed for some at least of the Queen's literary enthusiasm, Sir Kevin didn't care for him either. He was also irritated by his constant proximity because, while he was never actually in the room when the private secretary talked to the Queen, he was always within call.

They were discussing a royal visit to Wales due to take place in a fortnight's time. In the middle of being taken through her programme (a ride on a super-tram, a ukulele concert and a tour round a cheese factory), Her Majesty suddenly got up and went to the door.

'Norman.'

Sir Kevin heard a chair scrape as Norman got up.

'We're going to Wales in a few weeks' time.'

'Bad luck, ma'am.'

The Queen smiled back at the unsmiling Sir Kevin.

'Norman is so cheeky. Now we've read Dylan Thomas, haven't we, and some John Cowper Powys. And Jan Morris we've read. But who else is there?'

'You could try Kilvert, ma'am,' said Norman.

'Who's he?'

'A vicar, ma'am. Nineteenth century. Lived on the Welsh borders and wrote a diary. Fond of little girls.'

'Oh,' said the Queen, 'like Lewis Carroll.'

'Worse, ma'am.'

'Dear me. Can you get me the diaries?'

'I'll add them to our list, ma'am.'

Her Majesty closed the door and came back to her desk. 'You see, you can't say I don't do my homework, Sir Kevin.'

Sir Kevin, who had never heard of Kilvert, was unimpressed. The cheese factory is in a new business park, sited on reclaimed colliery land. It's revitalised the whole area.'

'Oh, I'm sure,' said the Queen. 'But you must admit that the literature is relevant.'

'I don't know that it is,' said Sir Kevin. 'The next-door factory where Your Majesty is opening the canteen makes computer components.'

'Some singing, I suppose?' said the Queen.

'There will be a choir, ma'am.'

'There generally is.'

Sir Kevin had a very muscular face, the Queen thought. He seemed to have muscles in his cheeks and when he frowned, they rippled. If she were a novelist, she thought, that might be worth writing down.

'We must make sure, ma'am, that we're singing from the same hymn sheet.'

'In Wales, yes. Most certainly. Any news from home? Busy shearing away?'

'Not at this time of year, ma'am.'

'Oh. Out to grass.'

She smiled the wide smile that indicated that the interview was over and when he turned to bow his head at the door she was already back in her book and without looking up simply murmured 'Sir Kevin' and turned the page.

SO IN DUE course Her Majesty went to Wales and to Scotland and to Lancashire and the West Country in that unremitting round of nationwide perambulation that is the lot of the monarch. The Queen must meet her people, however awkward and tongue-tied such meetings might turn out to be. Though it was here that her staff could help.

To get round the occasional speechlessness of her subjects when confronted with their sovereign the equerries would sometimes proffer handy hints as to possible conversations.

'Her Majesty may well ask you if you have had far to come. Have your answer ready and then possibly go on to say whether you came by train or by car. She may then ask you where you have left the car and whether the traffic was busier here than in – where did you say you came from? – Andover. The Queen, you see, is interested in all aspects of the nation's life, so she will sometimes talk about how difficult it is to park in London these days, which could take you on to a discussion of any parking problems you might have in Basingstoke.'

'Andover, actually, though Basingstoke's a nightmare too.'

'Quite so. But you get the idea? Small talk.'

Mundane though these conversations might be they had the merit of being predictable and above all brief, affording Her Majesty plenty of opportunities to cut the exchange short. The encounters ran smoothly and to a schedule, the Queen seemed interested and her subjects were seldom at a loss, and that perhaps the most eagerly anticipated conversation of their lives had only amounted to a discussion of the coned-off sections of the M6 hardly mattered. They had met the Queen and she had spoken to them and everyone got away on time.

So routine had such exchanges become that the equerries now scarcely bothered to invigilate them, hovering on the outskirts of the gathering always with a helpful if condescending smile. So it was only when it became plain that the tongue-tied quotient was increasing and that more and more of her subjects were at a loss when talking to Her Majesty that the staff began to eavesdrop on what was (or was not) being said.

It transpired that with no prior notification to her attendants the Queen had abandoned her long-standing lines of inquiry – length of service, distance travelled, place of origin – and had embarked on a new conversational gambit, namely, 'What are you reading at the moment?' To this very few of Her Majesty's loyal subjects had a ready answer (though one did try: 'The Bible?'). Hence the awkward pauses which the Queen tended to fill by saying, 'I'm reading...', sometimes even fishing in her handbag and giving them a glimpse of the lucky volume. Unsurprisingly the audiences got longer and more ragged, with a growing number of her loving subjects going away regretting that they had not performed well and feeling, too, that the monarch had somehow bowled them a googly.

Off duty, Piers, Tristram, Giles and Elspeth, all the Queen's devoted servants, compare notes: 'What are you reading? I mean, what sort of question is that? Most people, poor dears, aren't reading anything. Except if they say that, madam roots in her handbag, fetches out some volume she's just finished and makes them a present of it.'

'Which they promptly sell on eBay.'

'Quite. And have you been on a royal visit recently?' one of the ladies-in-waiting chips in. 'Because the word has got round. Whereas once upon a time the dear people would fetch along the odd daffodil or a bunch of mouldy old primroses which Her Majesty then passed back to us bringing up the rear, nowadays they fetch along books they're reading, or, wait for it, even writing, and if you're unlucky enough to be in attendance you practically need a trolley. If I'd wanted to cart books around I'd have got a job in Hatchards. I'm afraid Her Majesty is getting to be what is known as a handful.'

Still, the equerries accommodated, and disgruntled though they were at having to vary their routine, in the light of the Queen's new predilection her attendants reluctantly changed tack and in their pre-presentation warm-up now suggested that while Her Majesty might, as of old, still inquire as to how far the presentee had come and by what means, these days she was more likely to ask what the person was currently reading.

At this most people looked blank (and sometimes panicstricken) but, nothing daunted, the equerries came up with a list of suggestions.

Though this meant that the Queen came away with a disproportionate notion of the popularity of Andy McNab and the near universal affection for Joanna Trollope, no matter; at least embarrassment had been avoided. And once the answers had been supplied the audiences were back on track and finished on the dot as they used to do, the only hold-ups when, as seldom, one of her subjects confessed to a fondness for Virginia Woolf or Dickens, both of which provoked a lively (and lengthy) discussion. There were many who hoped for a similar meeting of minds by saying they were reading Harry Potter, but to this the Queen (who had no time for fantasy) invariably said briskly, 'Yes. One is saving that for a rainy day,' and passed swiftly on.

Seeing her almost daily meant that Sir Kevin was able to nag the Queen about what was now almost an obsession and to devise different approaches. 'I was wondering, ma'am, if we could somehow factor in your reading.' Once she would have let this pass, but one effect of reading had been to diminish the Queen's tolerance for jargon (which had always been low).

'Factor it in? What does that mean?'

'I'm just kicking the tyres on this one, ma'am, but it would help if we were able to put out a press release saying that, apart from English literature, Your Majesty was also reading ethnic classics.'

'Which ethnic classics did you have in mind, Sir Kevin? The Kama Sutra?'

Sir Kevin sighed.

'I am reading Vikram Seth at the moment. Would he count?'

Though the private secretary had never heard of him he thought he sounded right.

'Salman Rushdie?'

'Probably not, ma'am.'

'I don't see,' said the Queen, 'why there is any need for a press release at all. Why should the public care what I am reading? The Queen reads. That is all they need to know. "So what?" I imagine the general response.'

'To read is to withdraw. To make oneself unavailable. One would feel easier about it,' said Sir Kevin, 'if the pursuit itself were less... selfish.'

'Selfish?'

'Perhaps I should say solipsistic.'

'Perhaps you should.'

Sir Kevin plunged on. 'Were we able to harness your reading to some larger purpose – the literacy of the nation as a whole, for instance, the improvement of reading standards among the young...'

'One reads for pleasure,' said the Queen. 'It is not a public duty.'

'Perhaps,' said Sir Kevin, 'it should be.'

'Bloody cheek,' said the duke when she told him that night.

APROPOS THE duke, what of the family in all this? How did the Queen's reading impinge on them?

Had it been Her Majesty's responsibility to prepare meals, to shop or, unimaginably, to dust and hoover the house(s), standards would straightaway have been perceived to have fallen. But, of course, she had to do none of these things. That she did her boxes with less assiduity is true, but this didn't affect her husband or her children. What it did affect (or 'impact upon', as Sir Kevin put it) was the public sphere, where she had begun to perform her duties with a perceived reluctance: she laid foundation stones with less élan and what few ships there were to launch she sent down the slipway with no more ceremony than a toy boat on a pond, her book always waiting.

While this might concern her staff, her family were actually rather relieved. She had always kept them up to the mark and age had not made her more indulgent. Reading, though, had. She left the family more to themselves, chivvied them hardly at all and they had an easier time altogether. Hurray for books was their feeling, except when they were required to read them or when grandmama insisted on talking about them, quizzing them about their own reading habits or, worst of all, pressing books into their hands and checking later to see if they had been read.

As it was, they would often come upon her in odd unfrequented corners of her various dwellings, spectacles on the end of her nose, notebook and pencil beside her. She would glance up briefly and raise a vague, acknowledging hand. 'Well, I'm glad somebody's happy,' said the duke as he shuffled off down the corridor. And it was true; she was. She enjoyed reading like nothing else and devoured books at an astonishing rate, not that, Norman apart, there was anyone to be astonished.

Nor initially did she discuss her reading with anyone, least of all in public, knowing that such a late-flowering enthusiasm, however worthwhile, might expose her to ridicule. It would be the same, she thought, if she had developed a passion for God, or dahlias. At her age, people thought, why bother? To her, though, nothing could have been more serious, and she felt about reading what some writers felt about writing, that it was impossible not to do it and that at this late stage of her life she had been chosen to read as others were chosen to write.

To begin with, it's true, she read with trepidation and some unease. The sheer endlessness of books outfaced her and she had no idea how to go on; there was no system to her reading, with one book leading to another, and often she had two or three on the go at the same time. The next stage had been when she started to make notes, after which she always read with a pencil in hand, not summarising what she read but simply transcribing passages that struck her. It was only after a year or so of reading and making notes that she tentatively ventured on the occasional thought of her own. 'I think of literature,' she wrote, 'as a vast country to the far borders of which I am journeying but cannot possibly reach. And I have started too late. I will never catch up.' Then (an unrelated thought): 'Etiquette may be bad but embarrassment is worse.'

There was sadness to her reading, too, and for the first time in her life she felt there was a good deal she had missed. She had been reading one of the several lives of Sylvia Plath and was actually quite happy to have missed most of that, but reading the memoirs of Lauren Bacall she could not help feeling that Ms Bacall had had a much better bite at the carrot and, slightly to her surprise, found herself envying her for it.

That the Queen could readily switch from showbiz autobiography to the last days of a suicidal poet might seem both incongruous and wanting in perception. But, certainly in her early days, to her all books were the same and, as with her subjects, she felt a duty to approach them without prejudice. For her, there was no such thing as an improving book. Books were uncharted country and, to begin with at any rate, she made no distinction between them. With time came discrimination, but apart from the occasional word from Norman, nobody told her what to read, and what not. Lauren Bacall, Winifred Holtby, Sylvia Plath – who were they? Only by reading could she find out.

It was a few weeks later that she looked up from her book and said to Norman: 'Do you know that I said you were my amanuensis? Well, I've discovered what I am. I am an opsimath.'

With the dictionary always to hand, Norman read out: 'Opsimath: one who learns only late in life.'

It was this sense of making up for lost time that made her read with such rapidity and in the process now adding more frequent (and more confident) comments of her own, bringing to what was in effect literary criticism the same forthrightness with which she tackled other departments of her life. She was not a gentle reader and often wished authors were' around so that she could take them to task.

'Am I alone,' she wrote, 'in wanting to give Henry James a good talking-to?'

'I can see why Dr Johnson is well thought of, but surely, much of it is opinionated rubbish?'

It was Henry James she was reading one teatime when she said out loud, 'Oh, do get on.'

The maid, who was just taking away the tea trolley, said, 'Sorry, ma'am,' and shot out of the room in two seconds flat.

'Not you, Alice,' the Queen called after her, even

going to the door. 'Not you.'

Previously she wouldn't have cared what the maid thought or that she might have hurt her feelings, only now she did and coming back to the chair she wondered why. That this access of consideration might have something to do with books and even with the perpetually irritating Henry James did not at that moment occur to her.

Though the awareness of all the catching up she had to do never left her, her other regret was to do with all the famous authors she could have met but hadn't. In this respect at least she could mend her ways and she decided, partly at Norman's urging, that it would be interesting and even fun to meet some of the authors they had both been reading. Accordingly a reception was arranged, or a soiree, as Norman insisted on calling it.

The equerries naturally expected that the same form would apply as at the garden parties and other large receptions, with the tipping off of guests to whom Her Majesty was likely to stop and talk. The Queen, though, thought that on this occasion such formality was misplaced (these were artists after all) and decided to take pot luck. This turned out not to be a good idea.

Shy and even timid though authors had generally

seemed to be when she had met them individually, taken together they were loud, gossipy and, though they laughed a good deal, not, so far as she could tell, particularly funny. She found herself hovering on the edge of groups, with no one making much effort to include her, so that she felt like a guest at her own party. And when she did speak she either killed conversation and plunged it into an awful pause or the authors, presumably to demonstrate their independence and sophistication, took no notice at all of what she said and just went on talking.

It was exciting to be with writers she had come to think of as her friends and whom she longed to know. But now, when she was aching to declare her fellow feeling with those whose books she had read and admired, she found she had nothing to say. She, who had seldom in her life been intimidated by anyone, now found herself tongue-tied and awkward. 'I adored your book,' would have said it all, but fifty years of composure and self-possession plus half a century of understatement stood in the way. Hard put for conversation, she found herself falling back on some of her stock stand-bys. It wasn't quite 'How far did you have to come?' but their literary equivalent. 'How do you think of your characters? Do you work regular hours? Do you use a word-processor?' – questions which she knew were clichés and were embarrassing to inflict had the awkward silence not been worse.

One Scottish author was particularly alarming. Asked where his inspiration came from, he said fiercely: 'It doesn't come, Your Majesty. You have to go out and fetch it.'

When she did manage to express – and almost stammer – her admiration, hoping the author would tell her how he (the men, she decided, much worse than the women) had come to write the book in question, she found her enthusiasm brushed aside, as he insisted on talking not about the bestseller he had just written but about the one on which he was currently at work and how slowly it was going and how in consequence, as he sipped his champagne, he was the most miserable of creatures.

Authors, she soon decided, were probably best met with in the pages of their novels, and were as much creatures of the reader's imagination as the characters in their books. Nor did they seem to think one had done them a kindness by reading their writings. Rather they had done one the kindness by writing them.

To begin with she had thought she might hold such gatherings on a regular basis, but this soiree was enough to disabuse her of that. Once was enough. This came as a relief to Sir Kevin, who had not been enthusiastic, pointing out that if ma'am held an evening for the writers she would then have to hold a similar evening for the artists, and having held evenings for writers and artists the scientists would then expect to be entertained, too.

'Ma'am must not be seen to be partial.'

Well, there was now no danger of that.

With some justification, Sir Kevin blamed Norman for this evening of literary lacklustre, as he had encouraged the Queen when she had tentatively mentioned the idea. It wasn't as if Norman had had much of a time either. Literature being what it is the gay quotient among the guests was quite high, some of them asked along at Norman's specific suggestion. Not that that did him any good at all. Though like the other pages he was just taking round the drinks and the nibbles that went with them, Norman knew, as the others didn't, the reputation and standing of those whom he was bobbing up to with his tray. He had even read their books. But it was not Norman around whom they clustered, but the dolly pages and the loftier equerries who, as Norman said bitterly (though not to the Queen), wouldn't know a literary reputation if they stepped in it.

Still, if the whole experience of entertaining the Living Word was unfortunate, it did not (as Sir Kevin had hoped) put Her Majesty off reading. It turned her off wanting to meet authors, and to some extent off living authors altogether. But this just meant that she had more time for the dassies, for Dickens, Thackeray, George Eliot and the Brontës.

EVERY TUESDAY evening the Queen saw her prime minister, who briefed her on what he felt she ought to know. The press were fond of picturing these meetings as those of a wise and experienced monarch guiding her first minister past possible pitfalls and drawing on her unique repository of political experience accumulated over the fifty-odd years she had been on the throne in order to give him advice. This was a myth, though one in which the palace itself collaborated, the truth being the longer they were in office the less the prime ministers listened and the more they talked, the Queen nodding assent though not always agreement.

To begin with prime ministers wanted the Queen to hold their hand, and when they came to see her it was to be stroked and given an approving pat in the spirit of a child wanting to show its mother what it has done. And, as so often with her, it was really a show that was required, a show of interest, a show of concern. Men (and this included Mrs Thatcher) wanted show. At this stage, though, they still listened and even asked her advice, but as time passed all her prime ministers modulated with disturbing similarity into lecturing mode, when they ceased to require encouragement from the Queen but treated her like an audience, listening to her no longer on the agenda.

It was not only Gladstone who addressed the Queen as if she was a public meeting.

The audience this particular Tuesday had followed the usual pattern, and it was only when it was drawing to a close that the Queen managed to get a word in and talk about a subject that actually interested her. 'About my Christmas broadcast.'

'Yes, ma'am?' said the prime minister.

'I thought this year one might do something different.'

'Different, ma'am?'

'Yes. If one were to be sitting on a sofa reading or, even more informally, be discovered by the camera curled up with a book, the camera could creep in – is that the expression? – until I'm in mid-shot, when I could look up and say, "I've been reading this book about such and such," and then go on from there.'

'And what would the book be, ma'am?' The prime minister looked unhappy.

'That one would have to think about.'

'Something about the state of the world perhaps?' He brightened.

'Possibly, though they get quite enough of that from the newspapers. No. I was actually thinking of poetry.'

'Poetry, ma'am?' He smiled thinly.

'Thomas Hardy, for instance. I read an awfully good poem of his the other day about how the *Titanic* and the iceberg that was to sink her came together. It's called "The Convergence of the Twain". Do you know it?'

'I don't, ma'am. But how would it help?'

'Help whom?'

'Well' – and the prime minister seemed a trifle embarrassed actually to have to say it – 'the people.'

'Oh, surely,' said the Queen, 'it would show, wouldn't

it, that fate is something to which we are all subject.'

She gazed at the prime minister, smiling helpfully. He looked down at his hands.

'I'm not sure that is a message the government would feel able to endorse.' The public must not be allowed to think the world could not be managed. That way lay chaos. Or defeat at the polls, which was the same thing.

'I'm told' – and now it was his turn to smile helpfully – 'that there is some excellent footage of Your Majesty's visit to South Africa.'

The Queen sighed and pressed the bell. 'We will think about it.'

The prime minister knew that the audience was over as Norman opened the door and waited. 'So this,' thought the prime minister, 'is the famous Norman.'

'Oh, Norman,' said the Queen, 'the prime minister doesn't seem to have read Hardy. Perhaps you could find him one of our old paperbacks on his way out.'

Slightly to her surprise the Queen did after a fashion get her way, and though she was not curled up on the sofa but seated at her usual table, and though she did not read the Hardy poem (rejected as not 'forward-looking'), she began her Christmas broadcast with the opening paragraph of *A Tale of Two Cities* ('It was the best of times. It was the worst of times') and did it well, too. Choosing not to read from the autocue but from the book itself, she reminded the older ones in her audience (and they were the majority) of the kind of teacher some of them could still remember and who had read to them at school.

Encouraged by the reception given to her Christmas broadcast she persisted with her notion of reading in public, and late one night, as she dosed her book on the Elizabethan Settlement, it occurred to her to ring the Archbishop of Canterbury.

There was a pause while he turned down the TV.

'Archbishop. Why do I never read the lesson?'

'I beg your pardon, ma'am?'

'In church. Everybody else gets to read and one never does. It's not laid down, is it? It's not off-limits?'

'Not that I'm aware, ma'am.'

'Good. Well in that case I'm going to start. Leviticus, here I come. Goodnight.'

The archbishop shook his head and went back to *Strictly Come Dancing*.

But thereafter, particularly when she was in Norfolk, and even in Scotland, Her Majesty began to do a regular stint at the lectern. And not merely the lectern.

Visiting a Norfolk primary school she sat down on a classroom chair and read a story from Babar to the children. Addressing a City banquet she treated them to a Betjeman poem, impromptu departures from her schedule which enchanted everyone except Sir Kevin, from whom she hadn't bothered to get clearance.

Also unscheduled was the conclusion of a tree-planting ceremony. Having lightly dug an oak sapling into the reclaimed earth of a bleak urban farm above the Medway, she rested on the ceremonial spade and recited by heart Philip Larkin's poem 'The Trees', with its final verse:

> Yet still the unresting castles thresh
> In fullgrown thickness every May.
> Last year is dead, they seem to say,
> Begin afresh, afresh, afresh.

And as that dear and unmistakable voice carried over the shabby wind-bitten grass it seemed it was not just the huddled municipal party she was addressing but herself too. It was her life she was calling upon, the new beginning hers.

Still, though reading absorbed her, what' the Queen

had not expected was the degree to which it drained her of enthusiasm for anything else. It's true that at the prospect of opening yet another swimming-baths her heart didn't exactly leap up, but even so, she had never actually resented having to do it. However tedious her obligations had been – visiting this, conferring that – boredom had never come into it. This was her duty and when she opened her engagement book every morning it had never been without interest or expectation.

No more. Now she surveyed the unrelenting progression of tours, travels and undertakings stretching years into the future only with dread. There was scarcely a day she could call her own and never two. Suddenly it had all become a drag. 'Ma'am is tired,' said her maid, hearing her groan at her desk. 'It's time ma'am put her feet up occasionally.'

But it wasn't that. It was reading, and love it though she did, there were times when she wished she had never opened a book and entered into other lives. It had spoiled her. Or spoiled her for this, anyway.

MEANWHILE the grand visitors came and went, one

of them the president of France who proved such a let-down on the Genet front. She mentioned this to the foreign secretary in the debriefing that was customary after such visits, but he had never heard of the convict-playwright either. Still, she said, drifting rather from the comments the president had made about Anglo-French monetary arrangements, dead loss though he had been on Genet (whom he had dismissed as 'a denizen of the billiard hall'), he had proved a mine of information about Proust, who had hitherto just been a name to the Queen. To the foreign secretary he was not even that, and so she was able to fill him in a little.

'Terrible life, poor man. A martyr to asthma, apparently, and really someone to whom one would have wanted to say, "Oh do pull your socks up." But literature's full of those. The curious thing about him was that when he dipped his cake in his tea (disgusting habit) the whole of his past life came back to him. Well, I tried it and it had no effect on me at all. The real treat when I was a child was Fuller's cakes. I suppose it might work with me if I were to taste one of them, but of course they've long since gone out of business, so no memories there. Are we finished?' She reached for her book.

The Queen's ignorance of Proust was, unlike the

foreign secretary's, soon to be remedied, as Norman straightaway looked him up on the internet and, finding that the novel ran to thirteen volumes, thought it would be ideal reading on Her Majesty's summer holiday at Balmoral. George Painter's biography of Proust went with them, too. And seeing the blue-and pink-jacketed volumes ranged along her desk, the Queen thought they looked almost edible and straight out of a patisserie window.

It was a foul summer, cold, wet and unproductive, the guns grumbling every evening at their paltry bag. But for the Queen (and for Norman) it was an idyll. Seldom can there have been more of a contrast between the world of the book and the place in which it was read, the pair of them engrossed in the sufferings of Swann, the petty vulgarities of Mme Verdurin and the absurdities of Baron de Charlus, while in the wet butts on the hills the guns cracked out their empty tattoo and the occasional dead and sodden stag was borne past the window.

Duty required that the prime minister and his wife join the house party for a few days, and though not a shot himself he was at least hoping to accompany the Queen on some brisk walks through the heather where, as he put it, he 'hoped to get to know her better'. But knowing less of Proust than he did even of Thomas Hardy, the prime minister was disappointed: these would-be heart-to-hearts were never on the cards.

Breakfast over, Her Majesty retired to her study with Norman, the men drove off in their Land Rovers for another disappointing day and the prime minister and his wife were left to their own devices. Some days they trailed through the heather and over the moors to eat a wet and awkward picnic with the guns, but in the afternoon, having exhausted the area's shopping potential by buying a tweed rug and a box of shortbread, they could be found in a distant corner of the drawing room playing a sad game of Monopoly.

Four days of this was enough, and making an excuse ('trouble in the Middle East') the prime minister and his lady determined to depart early. On their last evening a game of charades was hurriedly organised, the choice of each well-known phrase or saying apparently one of the lesser-known prerogatives of the monarch, and well known though they may have been to her, they were a mystery to everyone else, including the prime minister.

The prime minister never liked to lose, even to the monarch, and it was no consolation to be told by one of the princes that no one but the Queen could hope to win, as the questions (several of them about Proust) were set by Norman and taken from their reading.

Had Her Majesty resumed a raft of long-disused prerogatives the prime minister could not have been more put out, and on his return to London he wasted no time in getting his special adviser on to Sir Kevin, who condoled with him, while pointing out that currently Norman was a burden they all had to share. The special adviser was unimpressed. 'Is this bloke Norman a nancy?'

Sir Kevin didn't know for certain but thought it was possible.

'And does she know that?'

'Her Majesty? Probably.'

'And do the press?'

'I think the press,' said Sir Kevin, clenching and unclenching his cheeks, 'are the last thing we want.'

'Exactly. So can I leave it with you?'

It happened that upcoming was a state visit to Canada, a treat that Norman was not down to share, preferring to go home for his holidays to Stockton-on-Tees. However, he made all the preparations beforehand, carefully packing a case of books that would see Her Majesty fully occupied from coast to farthest coast. The Canadians were not, so far as Norman knew, a bookish people and the schedule was so tight that the chances of Her Majesty getting to browse in a bookshop were slim. She was looking forward to the trip, as much of the journey was by train, and she pictured herself in happy seclusion whisked across the continent as she turned the pages of Pepys, whom she was reading for the first time.

In fact, though, the tour, or at least the beginning of it, turned out to be disastrous.

The Queen was bored, uncooperative and glum, shortcomings all of which her equerries would readily have blamed on her reading, were it not for the fact that, on this occasion, she had no reading, the books Norman had packed for her having unaccountably gone missing. Dispatched from Heathrow with the royal party, they turned up months later in Calgary, where they were made the focus of a nice if rather eccentric exhibition at the local library. In the meantime, though, Her Majesty had nothing to occupy her mind and rather than focusing her attention on the job in hand, which had been Sir Kevin's intention in arranging for the books' misdirection, being at a loose end just made her bad-tempered and difficult.

In the far north what few polar bears could be assembled hung about waiting for Her Majesty, but when she did not appear loped off to an ice floe that held more promise. Logs jammed, glaciers slid into the freezing waters, all unobserved by the royal visitor, who kept to her cabin.

'Don't you want to look at the St Lawrence Seaway?' said her husband.

'I opened it fifty years ago. I don't suppose it's changed.'

Even the Rockies received only a perfunctory glance and Niagara Falls was given a miss altogether ('I have seen it three times') and the duke went alone.

It happened, though, that at a reception for Canadian cultural notables the Queen got talking to Alice Munro and, learning that she was a novelist and short-story writer, requested one of her books, which she greatly enjoyed. Even better, it turned out there were many more where that came from and which Ms Munro readily supplied.

'Can there be any greater pleasure', she confided in her neighbour, the Canadian minister for overseas trade, 'than to come across an author one enjoys and then to find they have written not just one book or two, but at least a dozen?'

And all, though she did not say this, in paperback and so handbag size. A postcard was immediately dispatched to Norman telling him to get those few that were out of print from the library to await her return. Oh what treats!

But Norman was no longer there.

THE DAY before he was due to depart for the delights of Stockton-on-Tees Norman was called into Sir Kevin's office. The prime minister's special adviser had said that Norman should be sacked; Sir Kevin disliked the special adviser; he didn't like Norman much but he disliked the special adviser more, and it was this that saved Norman's bacon. Besides, Sir Kevin felt the sack was vulgar. Norman should not get the sack. There was a neater solution.

'Her Majesty is always anxious for the betterment of her employees,' the private secretary said benignly, 'and though she is more than satisfied with your work she wonders if you have ever thought of university?'

'University?' said Norman, who hadn't.

'Specifically, the University of East Anglia. They have a very good English Department and indeed a School of Creative Writing. I have only to mention the names' – Sir Kevin looked down at his pad – 'of Ian McEwan, Rose Tremain and Kazuo Ishiguro...'

'Yes,' said Norman. 'We've read those.'

Wincing at the 'we', the private secretary said that he thought East Anglia would suit Norman very well.

'What with?' said Norman. 'I've no money.'

'That will not be a problem. Her Majesty, you see, is anxious not to hold you back.'

'I think I would rather stay here,' said Norman. 'It's an education in itself.'

'Ye-es,' said the private secretary. 'That will not be possible. Her Majesty has someone else in mind. Of course,' he smiled helpfully, 'your job in the kitchen is always open.'

Thus it was that when the Queen returned from Canada there was no Norman perched on his usual seat in the corridor. His chair was empty, not that there was a chair any more or that comforting pile of books she had got used to finding on her bedside table. More immediately, there was no one to whom she could discourse on the excellences of Alice Munro.

'He wasn't popular, ma'am,' said Sir Kevin.

'He was popular with me,' said the Queen. 'Where has he gone?'

'No idea, ma'am.'

Norman, being a sensitive boy, wrote the Queen a long, chatty letter about the courses he was taking and the reading he had to do, but when he got a reply beginning 'Thank you for your letter in which Her Majesty was most interested' he knew he had been eased out, though whether by the Queen or her private secretary he wasn't sure.

If Norman didn't know who had engineered his departure, the Queen herself was in no doubt. Norman had gone the way of the travelling library and the case of books that ended up in Calgary. Like the book she had hidden behind the cushion in the state coach, he was lucky not to have been exploded. And she missed him, there was no doubt. But no letter came, no note, and there was nothing for it but grimly to go on. It wouldn't put a stop to her reading.

That the Queen was not more troubled by Norman's sudden departure might seem surprising and to reflect poorly on her character. But sudden absences and abrupt departures had always been a feature of her life.

She was seldom told, for instance, when anyone was ill; distress and even fellow feeling something that being Queen entitled her to be without, or so her courtiers thought. When, as unfortunately happened, death did claim a servant or even sometimes a friend, it was often the first time that the Queen had heard that anything was amiss, 'We mustn't worry Her Majesty' a guiding principle for all her servants.

Norman of course had not died, just gone to the University of East Anglia, though, as the equerries saw it, this was much the same thing, as he had gone from Her Majesty's life and thus no longer existed, his name never mentioned by the Queen or anyone else. But the Queen should not be blamed on that score, on that the equerries agreed; the Queen should never be blamed. People died, people left and (more and more) people got into the papers. For her they were all departures of one sort or another. They left but she went on.

Less to her credit, before Norman's mysterious departure the Queen had begun to wonder if she was outgrowing him ... or rather, out-reading him. Once upon a time he had been a humble and straightforward guide to the world of books. He had advised her as to what to read and had not hesitated to say when he thought she was not ready for a book yet. Beckett, for instance, he had kept from her for a long while, and Nabokov, and it was only gradually he had introduced her to Philip Roth (with *Portnoy's Complaint* quite late on in the sequence).

More and more, though, she had read what she fancied and Norman had done the same. They talked about what they were reading but increasingly she felt her life and experience gave her the advantage; books could only take one so far. She had learned, too, that Norman's preferences could sometimes be suspect. Other things being equal he still tended to prefer gay authors, hence her acquaintance with Genet. Some she liked – the novels of Mary Renault, for instance, fascinated her – but others of a deviant persuasion she was less keen on: Denton Welch, for instance (a favourite of Norman's), whom she felt was rather unhealthy; Isherwood (no time for all the meditation). As a reader she was brisk and straightforward; she didn't want to *wallow* in anything.

With no Norman to talk to, the Queen now found she was conducting lengthier discussions with herself and putting more and more of her thoughts on paper, so that her notebooks multiplied and widened in scope. 'One recipe for happiness is to have no sense of entitlement.' To this she added a star and noted at the bottom of the page: 'This is not a lesson I have ever been in a position to learn.'

'I was giving the CH once, I think it was to Anthony Powell, and we were discussing bad behaviour. Notably well behaved himself and even conventional, he remarked that being a writer didn't excuse one from being a human being. Whereas (one didn't say this) being Queen does. I have to seem like a human being all the time, but I seldom have to be one. I have people to do that for me.'

In addition to thoughts such as these she found herself noting descriptions of people she met, not necessarily all of them famous: their oddities of behaviour, their turns of phrase, as well as the stories she was told, often in confidence. When some scandalous report about the royal family appeared in the newspapers the real facts went into her notebook. When some scandal escaped public notice, that too went down, and all of them told in that sensible, down-to-earth tone of voice she was coming to recognise and even relish as her own style.

In the absence of Norman her reading, though it

did not falter, did change direction. While she still ordered books from the London Library and from booksellers, with Norman gone it was no longer their secret. Now she had to ask the lady-in-waiting, who spoke to the comptroller before drawing the petty cash. It was a wearisome process, which she would occasionally circumvent by asking one of the more peripheral grandchildren to get her books. They were happy to oblige and pleased to be taken notice of at all, the public scarcely knowing they existed. But more and more now the Queen began to take books out of her own libraries, particularly the one at Windsor, where, though the choice of modern books was not unlimited, the shelves were stacked with many editions of the classic texts, some of them, of course, autographed – Balzac, Turgenev, Fielding, Conrad, books which once she would have thought beyond her but which now she sailed through, pencil always in hand, and in the process, incidentally, becoming reconciled even to Henry James, whose divagations she now took in her stride: 'After all,' as she wrote in her notebook, 'novels are not necessarily written as the crow flies.' Seeing her sitting at the window to catch the last of the light, the librarian thought that a more assiduous reader these ancient shelves had not seen since the days of George Ⅲ .

The librarian at Windsor had been one of many who had urged on Her Majesty the charms of Jane Austen, but being told on all sides how much ma'am would like her put ma'am off altogether. Besides she had handicaps as a reader of Jane Austen that were peculiarly her own. The essence of Jane Austen lies in minute social distinctions, distinctions which the Queen's unique position made it difficult for her to grasp. There was such a chasm between the monarch and even her grandest subject that the social differences beyond that were somewhat telescoped. So the social distinctions of which Jane Austen made so much seemed of even less consequence to the Queen than they did to the ordinary reader, thus making the novels much harder going. To begin with at any rate Jane Austen was practically a work of entomology, the characters not quite ants but seeming to the royal reader so much alike as to require a microscope. It was only as she gained in understanding both of literature and of human nature that they took on individuality and charm.

Feminism, too, got short shrift, at least to begin with and for the same reason, the separations of gender like the differences of class as nothing compared with the gulf that separated the Queen from the rest of humanity.

But whether it was Jane Austen or feminism or even Dostoevsky the Queen eventually got round to it and to much else besides, but never without regret. Years ago she had sat next to Lord David Cecil at a dinner in Oxford and had been at a loss for conversation. He, she found, had written books on Jane Austen and these days she would have relished the encounter. But Lord David was dead and so it was too late. Too late. It was all too late. But she went on, determined as ever and always trying to catch up.

THE HOUSEHOLD, too, went on, running as smoothly as it always did, the moves from London to Windsor to Norfolk to Scotland achieved with no seeming effort, at any rate on her part, so that sometimes she felt almost surplus to the procedure, the same transferences and translations accomplished regardless of the person at their centre. It was a ritual of departure and arrival in which she was just a piece of luggage; the most important piece, there was no disputing that, but luggage nevertheless.

In one respect these peregrinations went better than they had done in the past, in that the personage around whom they revolved generally had her nose in a book. She got into the car at Buckingham Palace and got out at Windsor without ever leaving the side of Captain Crouchback in the evacuation of Crete. She flew to Scotland happy in the (occasionally exasperating) company of Tristram Shandy, and when she got bored with him Trollope (Anthony) was never far away. It all made her a pliant and undemanding traveller. True, she wasn't always quite as on the dot as she used to be, and the motor waiting under the canopy in the courtyard was a familiar sight, the duke increasingly tetchy in the back. But when she eventually hurried into the car she was never tetchy; after all, she had her book.

Her household, though, had no such solace and the equerries in particular were becoming increasingly restive and critical. Urbane and exquisitely mannered though he is, the equerry is essentially only a stage manager; always aware when deference is due he (or occasionally she) knows, too, that this is a performance and he is in charge of it, with Her Majesty playing the leading role.

The audience or the spectators – and where the Queen is concerned everyone is a spectator – know that it is a performance, while liking to tell themselves that it isn't, quite, and to think, performance notwithstanding, that they have occasionally caught a glimpse of behaviour that is more 'natural', more 'real' – the odd overheard remark, for instance ('I could murder a gin and tonic,' from the late Queen Mother, 'Bloody dogs,' from the Duke of Edinburgh), or the Queen sitting down at a garden party and thankfully kicking off her shoes. In truth, of course, these supposedly unguarded moments are just as much a performance as the royal family at its most hieratic. This show, or sideshow, might be called playing at being normal and is as contrived as the most formal public appearance, even though those who witness or overhear it think that this is the Queen and her family at their most human and natural. Formal or informal, it is all part of that self-presentation in which the equerries collaborate and which, these apparently impromptu moments apart, is from the public's point of view virtually seamless.

It only gradually came home to the equerries that these supposedly sincere moments, glimpses of the Queen as she 'really is', were occurring less often.

Diligently though Her Majesty might carry out all her duties, that was all she was doing, and never now pretending, as it were, to break ranks and seldom coming out with supposedly unrehearsed remarks ('Careful,' she might say as she pins a medal on a young man, 'I don't want to stab you through the heart'), remarks that could be taken home and cherished, along with the invitation card, the special car-park pass and the map of the palace precincts.

These days she was formal, smiling and seemingly sincere but without frills and with none of the supposedly off-the-cuff asides with which she was wont to enliven the proceedings. 'Poor show,' thought the equerries and that is exactly what they meant, 'a poor show' in which Her Majesty had turned in a dull performance. But they were not in a position to draw attention to this omission as they, too, colluded in the pretence that such moments were natural and unpremeditated, a genuine overflowing of Her Majesty's sense of fun.

It had been an investiture.

'Less spontaneous this morning, ma'am,' one of the bolder equerries ventured to say.

'Was I?' said the Queen, who would once have been

most put out at even this mildest of criticisms, though these days it scarcely impinged. 'I think I know why it is. You see, Gerald, as they kneel one looks down on the tops of people's heads a good deal and from that perspective even the most unsympathetic personality seems touching: the beginnings of a bald patch, the hair growing over the collar. One's feelings are almost maternal.'

The equerry, with whom she'd never shared such confidences before and who ought to have been flattered, simply felt awkward and embarrassed. This was a truly human side to the monarch of which he'd never been previously aware and which (unlike its counterfeit versions) he did not altogether welcome. And whereas the Queen herself thought that such feelings probably arose out of her reading books, the young man felt it might be that she was beginning to show her age. Thus it was that the dawn of sensibility was mistaken for the onset of senility.

Immune to embarrassment herself, as she was to any that she might cause, the Queen would once not have noticed the young man's confusion. But observing it now she resolved in the future to share her thoughts less promiscuously, which was a pity in a way as it was what many in the nation longed for. Instead she determined to restrict her confidences to her notebooks, where they could do no harm.

The Queen had never been demonstrative; it was not in her upbringing; but more and more these days, particularly in the period following Princess Diana's death, she was being required to go public about feelings she would have preferred to keep to herself. At that time, though, she had not yet begun to read, and it was only now that she understood that her predicament was not unique and that she shared it, among others, with Cordelia. She wrote in her notebook: 'Though I do not always understand Shakespeare, Cordelia's "I cannot heave my heart into my mouth" is a sentiment I can readily endorse. Her predicament is mine.'

Though the Queen was always discreet about writing in her notebooks her equerry was not reassured. He had once or twice caught her at it and thought that this, too, pointed to potential derangement. What had Her Majesty to note down? She never used to do it and like any change of behaviour in the elderly it was readily put down to decay.

'Probably Alzheimer's,' said another of the young men. 'You have to write things down for them, don't you?' and this, taken together with Her Majesty's growing indifference to appearances, made her attendants fear the worst.

That the Queen might be thought to be suffering from Alzheimer's disease was shocking in the obvious way, the 'human' and compassionate way, but to Gerald and the other equerries it was more subtly deplorable. It seemed to him pitiable that Her Majesty, whose life had always been so sequestered, should now have to share this undignified depletion with so many of her subjects, her deterioration, he felt, deserving a royal enclosure where her behavior (and that of monarchs generally) might be allowed a larger degree of latitude and even waywardness before it attracted the levelling denomination of Alzheimer and his all-too-common disease. It could have been a syllogism, if Gerald had known what a syllogism was: Alzheimer's is common, the Queen is not common, therefore the Queen has not got Alzheimer's.

Nor had she, of course, and in fact her faculties had never been sharper and unlike her equerry she would certainly have known what a syllogism was.

Besides, apart from writing in her notebooks and her now fairly customary lateness, what did this deterioration amount to? A brooch repeated, say, or a pair of court shoes worn on successive days: the truth was Her Majesty didn't care, or didn't care as much, and herself not caring, her attendants, being human, began to care less, too, cutting corners as the Queen would never previously have countenanced. The Queen had always dressed with great care. She had an encyclopaedic knowledge of her wardrobe and her multiple accessories and was scrupulous in ringing the changes on her various outfits. No longer. An ordinary woman who wore the same frock twice in a fortnight would not be thought slipshod or negligent of appearances. But in the Queen, the permutations of whose wardrobe were worked out down to the last buckle, such repetitions signalled a dramatic falling away from her own self-imposed standards of decorum.

'Doesn't ma'am care?' said the maid boldly.

'Care about what?' said the Queen, which, while being an answer of sorts, did nothing to reassure the maid, convincing her that something was deeply amiss, so that like the equerries her personal attendants began to prepare for a lengthy decline.

STILL, THOUGH he saw her every week, the occasional want of variation in the Queen's attire and the sameness of her earrings went unnoticed by the prime minister.

It had not always been so, and at the start of his term of office he had frequently complimented the Queen on what Her Majesty was wearing and her always discreet jewellery. He was younger then, of course, and thought of it as flirting, though it was also a form of nerves. She was younger, too, but she was not nervous and had been long enough at the game to know that this was just a phase that most prime ministers went through (the exceptions being Mr Heath and Mrs Thatcher) and that as the novelty of their weekly interviews diminished so, too, did the flirting.

It was another aspect of the myth of the Queen and her prime minister, the decline of the prime minister's attention to her personal appearance coinciding with his dwindling concern with what Her Majesty had to say, how the Queen looked and how the Queen thought, both of diminishing importance, so that, earrings or no earrings, making her occasional comments she felt not unlike an air hostess going through the safety procedures, the look on the prime minister's face that of benevolent and minimal attention from a passenger who has heard it all before.

The inattention, though, and the boredom were not all his, and as she had begun to read more, she resented the time these meetings took up and so thought to enliven the process by relating them to her studies and what she was learning about history.

This was not a good idea. The prime minister did not wholly believe in the past or in any lessons that might be drawn from it. One evening he was addressing her on the subject of the Middle East when she ventured to say, 'It is the cradle of civilisation, you know.'

'And shall be again, ma'am,' said the prime minister, 'provided we are allowed to persist,' and then bolted off down a side alley about the mileage of new sewage pipes that had been laid and the provision of electricity substations.

She interrupted again. 'One hopes this isn't to the detriment of the archaeological remains. Do you know about Ur?'

He didn't. So as he was going she found him a couple of books that might help. The following week she asked him if he had read them (which he hadn't).

'They were most interesting, ma'am.'

'Well, in that case we must find you some more. I

find it fascinating.'

This time Iran came up and she asked him if he knew of the history of Persia, or Iran (he had scarcely even connected the two), and gave him a book on that besides, and generally began to take such an interest that after two or three sessions like this, Tuesday evenings, which he had hitherto looked forward to as a restful oasis in his week, now became fraught with apprehension. She even questioned him about the books as if they were homework. Finding he hadn't read them she smiled tolerantly.

'My experience of prime ministers, Prime Minister, is that, with Mr Macmillan the exception, they prefer to have their reading done for them.'

'One is busy, ma'am,' said the prime minister.

'One is busy,' she agreed and reached for her book. 'We will see you next week.'

Eventually Sir Kevin got a call from the special adviser.

'Your employer has been giving my employer a hard time.'

'Yes?'

'Yes. Lending him books to read. That's out of order.'

'Her Majesty likes reading.'

'I like having my dick sucked. I don't make the prime minister do it. Any thoughts, Kevin?'

'I will speak to Her Majesty.'

'You do that, Kev. And tell her to knock it off.'

Sir Kevin did not speak to Her Majesty, still less tell her to knock it off. Instead, swallowing his pride, he went to see Sir Claude.

IN THE little garden of his delightful seventeenth-century grace-and-favour cottage at Hampton Court Sir Claude Pollington was reading. Actually, he was meant to be reading, but he was dozing over a box of confidential documents sent over from the library at Windsor, a privilege accorded to him as an ancient royal servant, now ninety at least but still ostensibly working on his memoirs, tentatively entitled 'Drudgery Divine'.

Sir Claude had entered royal service straight from Harrow at the age of eighteen as a page to George V, one of his first tasks, as he was fond of recalling, being to lick the hinges with which that testy and punctilious monarch used to stick the stamps into his many albums. 'Were there a problem discovering my DNA,' he had once confided to Sue Lawley, 'one would only have to look behind the stamps in dozens of the royal albums, particularly, I recall, the stamps of Tanna Touva, which His Majesty thought vulgar and even common but which he nevertheless felt obliged to collect. Which was typical of His Majesty ... conscientious to a fault.' He had then chosen a record of Master Ernest Lough singing 'O for the Wings of a Dove'.

In his little drawing room every surface sprouted framed photographs of the various royals whom Sir Claude had so loyally served. Here he was at Ascot, holding the King's binoculars; crouching in the heather as His Majesty drew a bead on a distant stag. This was him bringing up the rear as Queen Mary emerged from a Harrogate antique shop, the young Pollington's face hidden behind a parcel containing a Wedgwood vase, reluctantly bestowed on Her Majesty by the hapless dealer. Here he was, too, in a striped jersey, helping to crew the *Nahlin* on that fateful Mediterranean cruise, the lady in the yachting cap a Mrs Simpson – a photograph that tended to come and go, and which was never on view when, as often used to happen, Queen Elizabeth the Queen Mother dropped in for tea.

There was not much about the royal family to which Sir Claude had not been privy. After his service with

George V he had been briefly in the household of Edward VIII and moved smoothly on into the service of his brother, George VI. He had done duty in many of the offices of the household, finally serving as private secretary to the Queen. Even when he had long retired his advice was frequently called on; he was a living embodiment of that establishment commendation, 'a safe pair of hands'.

Now, though, his hands shook rather and he was not as careful as he used to be about personal hygiene, and even sitting with him in the fragrant garden Sir Kevin had to catch his breath.

'Should we go inside?' said Sir Claude. 'There could be tea.'

'No, no,' said Sir Kevin hastily. 'Here is better.'

He explained the problem.

'Reading?' said Sir Claude, 'No harm in that, surely? Her Majesty takes after her namesake, the first Elizabeth. She was an avid reader. Of course, there were fewer books then. And Queen Elizabeth the Queen Mother, she liked a book. Queen Maiy didn't, of course. Or George V. He was a great stamp collector. That's how I started, you know. Licking his hinges.'

Someone even older than Sir Claude brought out tea,

which Sir Kevin prudently poured.

'Her Majesty is very fond of you, Sir Claude.'

'As I am of her,' said the old man. 'I have been in thrall to Her Majesty since she was a girl. All my life.'

And it had been a distinguished life, too, with a good war in which the young Pollington won several medals and commendations for bravery, serving finally on the general staff.

'I've served three queens,' he was fond of saying, 'and got on with them all. The only queen I could never get on with was Field Marshal Montgomeiy.'

'She listens to you,' said Sir Kevin, wondering if the sponge cake was reliable.

'I like to think so,' said Sir Claude. 'But what do I say? Reading. How curious. Tuck in.'

Just in time Sir Kevin realised that what he had taken for frosting was in fact mould and he managed to palm the cake into his briefcase.

'Perhaps you could remind her of her duty?'

'Her Majesty has never needed to be reminded of that. Too much duty if you ask me. Let me think ...'

And the old man pondered while Sir Kevin waited.

It was some time before he realised that Sir Claude was asleep. He got up loudly.

'I will come,' said Sir Claude. 'It's a bit since I had an outing. You'll send a car?'

'Of course,' said Sir Kevin, shaking hands. 'Don't get up.'

As he went Sir Claude called after him.

'You're the New Zealand one, aren't you?'

'I GATHER,' said the equerry, 'that it might be advisable if Your Majesty were to see Sir Claude in the garden.'

'In the garden?'

'Out of doors, ma'am. In the fresh air.'

The Queen looked at him. 'Do you mean he smells?'

'Apparently he does rather, ma'am.'

'Poor thing.' She wondered sometimes where they thought she'd been all her life. 'No. He must come up here.'

Though when the equerry offered to open a window she did not demur.

'What does he want to see me about?'

'I've no idea, ma'am.'

Sir Claude came in on his two sticks, bowing his head at the door and again when Her Majesty gave him her hand as she motioned him to sit down. Though her smile remained kindly and her manner unchanged, the equerry had not exaggerated.

'How are you, Sir Claude?'

'Very well, Your Majesty. And you, ma'am?'

'Very well.'

The Queen waited, but too much the courtier to introduce a subject unprompted Sir Claude waited too.

'What was it you wanted to see me about?'

While Sir Claude tried to remember, the Queen had time to notice the thin reef of dandruff that had gathered beneath his coat collar, the egg stains on his tie and the drift of scurf that lay in his large pendulous ear. Whereas once upon a time such frailties would have been beneath her notice and gone unremarked now they obtruded on her gaze, ruffling her composure and even causing her distress. Poor man. And he had fought at Tobruk. She must write it down.

'Reading, ma'am.'

'I beg your pardon.'

'Your Majesty has started reading.'

'No, Sir Claude. One has always read. Only these days one is reading more.'

Now, of course, she knew why he had come and who

had put him up to it, and from being an object wholly of pity this witness to half her life now took his place among her persecutors; all compassion fled and she recovered her composure.

'I see no harm in reading in itself, ma'am.'

'One is relieved to hear it.'

'It's when it's carried to extremes. There's the mischief.'

'Are you suggesting one rations one's reading?'

'Your Majesty has led such an exemplary life. That it should be reading that has taken Your Majesty's fancy is almost by the way. Had you invested any pursuit with similar fervour eyebrows must have been raised.'

'They might. But then one has spent one's life not raising eyebrows. One feels sometimes that that is not much of a boast.'

'Ma'am has always liked racing.'

'True, Only one's rather gone off it at the moment.'

'Oh,' said Sir Claude. 'That's a shame.' Then, seeing a possible accommodation between racing and reading, 'Her Majesty the Queen Mother used to be a big fan of Dick Francis.'

'Yes,' said the Queen. 'I've read one or two, though they only take one so far. Swift, I discover, is very good about horses.'

Sir Claude nodded gravely, not having read Swift and reflecting that he seemed to be getting nowhere.

They sat for a moment in silence, but it was long enough for Sir Claude to fall asleep. This had seldom happened to the Queen and when it had (a government minister nodding off alongside her at some ceremony, for instance) her reaction had been brisk and unsympathetic. She was often tempted to fall asleep, as with her job who wouldn't be, but now, rather than wake the old man she just waited, listening to his laboured breathing and wondering hpw long it would be before infirmity overtook her and she became similarly incapable. Sir Claude had come with a message, she understood that and resented it, but perhaps he was a message in his own person, a portent of the unpalatable future.

She picked up her notebook from the desk and dropped it on the floor. Sir Claude woke up nodding and smiling as if appreciating something the Queen had just said.

'How are your memoirs?' said the Queen. Sir Claude's memoirs had been on the go for so long they had become a joke in the household. 'How far have you got?'

'Oh, they're not consecutive, ma'am. One does a little every day.'

He didn't, of course, and it was really only to forestall yet another probing royal question that he now said what he did. 'Has Your Majesty ever considered writing?'

'No,' said the Queen, though this was a lie. 'Where would one find the time?'

'Ma'am has found time for reading.'

This was a rebuke and the Queen did not take kindly to rebukes, but for the moment she overlooked it.

'What should one write?'

'Your Majesty has had an interesting life.'

'Yes,' said the Queen. 'One has.'

The truth was Sir Claude had no notion of what the Queen should write or whether she should write at all, and he had only suggested writing in order to get her off reading and because in his experience writing seldom got done. It was a cul-de-sac. He had been writing his memoirs for twenty years and hadn't even written fifty pages.

'Yes,' he said firmly. 'Ma'am must write. But can I give Your Majesty a tip? Don't start at the beginning.

That's the mistake I made. Start off in the middle. Chronology is a great deterrent.'

'Was there anything else, Sir Claude?'

The Queen gave her wide smile. The interview was over. How the Queen conveyed this information had always been a mystery to Sir Claude, but it was as plain as if a bell had rung. He struggled to his feet as the equerry opened the door, bowed his head, then when he reached the door turned and bowed his head again, then slowly stumped down the corridor on his two sticks, one of them a present from the Queen Mother.

Back in the room the Queen opened the window wider and let the breeze blow in from the garden. The equerry returned, and raising her eyebrows the Queen indicated the chair on which Sir Claude had been sitting, now with a damp patch staining the satin. Silently the young man bore the chair away, while the Queen gathered up her book and her cardigan preparatory to going into the garden.

By the time the equerry returned with another chair she had stepped out onto the terrace. He put it down and with the skill of long practice quickly set the room to rights, spotting as he did so the Queen's notebook lying on the floor. He picked it up and before replacing it on the desk stood for a moment wondering in the Queen's absence if he might take a peep at the contents. Except at that moment Her Majesty reappeared in the doorway.

'Thank you, Gerald,' she said and held out her hand.

He gave her the book and she went out.

'Shit,' said Gerald. 'Shit. Shit. Shit.'

This note of self-reproach was not inappropriate as within days Gerald was no longer in attendance on Her Majesty and indeed no longer in the household at all, but back with his scarcely remembered regiment yomping in the rain over the moors of Northumberland. The speed and ruthlessness of his almost Tudor dispatch sent, as Sir Kevin would have put it, the right message and at least put paid to any further rumours of senile decay. Her Majesty was herself again.

NOTHING Sir Claude had said carried any weight, but still she found herself thinking about it that evening at the Royal Albert Hall, where there was a special promenade concert in her honour. In the past music had never been much of a solace and had always been tinged with obligation, the repertoire familiar largely from concerts like this she had had to attend. Tonight, though, the music seemed more relevant.

This was a voice, she thought, as a boy played the clarinet: Mozart, a voice everybody in the hall knew and recognised though Mozart had been dead two hundred years. And she remembered Helen Schlegel in Howards End putting pictures to Beethoven at the concert in the Queen's Hall that Forster describes, Beethoven's another voice that everyone knew.

The boy finished, the audience applauded and, clapping too, she leaned over towards another of the party as if sharing her appreciation. But what she wanted to say was that, old as she was, renowned as she was, no one knew her voice. And in the car taking them back she suddenly said: 'I have no voice.'

'Not surprised,' said the duke. 'Too damned hot. Throat, is it?'

It was a sultry night and unusually for her she woke in the early hours unable to sleep.

The policeman in the garden, seeing the light go on, turned on his mobile as a precaution.

She had been reading about the Brontes and what a hard time they had had of it when they were children, but she didn't feel that would send her off to sleep again and, looking for something else, saw in the corner of the bookshelf the book by Ivy Compton-Burnett which she had borrowed from the travelling library and which Mr Hutchings had given her all that time ago. It had been hard going and had nearly sent her to sleep then, she remembered, so perhaps it would do the trick again.

Far from it, and the novel she had once found slow now seemed refreshingly brisk, dry still but astringently so, with Dame Ivy's no-nonsense tone reassuringly close to her own. And it occurred to her (as next day she wrote down) that reading was, among other things, a muscle and one that she had seemingly developed. She could read the novel with ease and great pleasure, laughing at remarks (they were hardly jokes) that she had not even noticed before. And through it all she could hear the voice of Ivy Compton Burnett, unsentimental, severe and wise. She could hear her voice as clearly as earlier in the evening she had heard the voice of Mozart. She closed the book. And once again she said out loud: 'I have no voice.'

And somewhere in West London where these things are recorded a transcribing and expressionless typist thought it was an odd remark and said as if in reply: 'Well, if you don't, dear, I don't know who does.'

Back in Buckingham Palace the Queen waited a moment or two, then switched off the light, and under the catalpa tree in the grounds the policeman saw the light go out and turned off his mobile.

In the darkness it came to the Queen that, dead, she would exist only in the memories of people. She who had never been subject to anyone would now be on a par with everybody else. Reading could not change that – though writing might.

Had she been asked if reading had enriched her life she would have had to say yes, undoubtedly, though adding with equal certainty that it had at the same time drained her life of all purpose. Once she had been a self-assured single-minded woman knowing where her duty lay and intent on doing it for as long as she was able. Now all too often she was in two minds. Reading was not doing, that had always been the trouble. And old though she was she was still a doer.

She switched the light on again and reached for her notebook and wrote: 'You don't put your life into your books. You find it there.'

Then she went to sleep.

IN THE WEEKS that followed it was noticeable that

the Queen was reading less, if at all. She was pensive and abstracted even, but not because her mind was on what she was reading. She no longer carried a book with her wherever she went and the piles of volumes that had accumulated on her desk were shelved, sent back to the libraries or otherwise dispersed.

But, reading or not, she still spent long hours at her desk, sometimes looking at her notebooks and occasionally writing in them, though she knew, without quite spelling it out to herself, that her writing would be even less popular than her reading, and did anyone knock at the door she immediately swept them into her desk drawer before saying, 'Come in.'

She found, though, that when she had written something down, even if it was just an entry in her notebook, she was happy as once she would have been happy after doing some reading. And it came to her again that she did not want simply to be a reader. A reader was next door to being a spectator whereas when she was writing she was doing, and doing was her duty.

Meanwhile she was often in the library, particularly at Windsor, looking through her old desk diaries, the albums of her innumerable visits, her archive in fact.

'Is there anything specific that Your Majesty is

looking for?' said the librarian after he had brought her yet another pile of material.

'No,' said the Queen. 'One is just trying to remember what it was like. Though what "it" is one isn't sure either.'

'Well, if Your Majesty does remember, then I hope you will tell me. Or better still, ma'am, write it down. Your Majesty is a living archive.'

Though she felt he could have expressed this more tactfully, she knew what he meant and reflected, too, that here was someone else who was urging her to write. It was almost becoming a duty, and she had always been very good at duty, until, that is, she started to read. Still, to be urged to write and to be urged to publish are two different things and nobody so far was urging her to do the latter.

Seeing the books disappear from her desk and having once more something approaching Her Majesty's whole attention were welcome to Sir Kevin and indeed to the household in general. Timekeeping did not improve, it's true, and the Queen's wardrobe still tended to be a little wayward ('I'd outlaw that cardigan,' said her maid). But Sir Kevin shared in the general impression that for all these persistent shortcomings Her Majesty had seen off her infatuation with books and had returned to normal.

She stayed that autumn for a few days at Sandringham, as she was scheduled to make a royal visit to the city of Norwich. There was a service in the cathedral, a walkabout in the pedestrian precinct and before she had luncheon at the university she opened a new fire station.

Seated between the vice-chancellor and the professor of creative writing she was mildly surprised when over her shoulder came a bony wrist and red hand that were very familiar, proffering a prawn cocktail.

'Hello, Norman.' she said.

'Your Majesty,' said Norman correctly, and smoothly presented the lord lieutenant with his prawn cocktail, before going on down the table.

'Your Majesty knows Seakins then, ma'am?' said the professor of creative writing.

'One did,' said the Queen, saddened a little that Norman seemed to have made no progress in the world at all and was seemingly back in a kitchen, even if it was not hers.

'We thought,' said the vice-chancellor, 'that it would be rather a treat for the students if they were to serve the meal. They will be paid, of course, and it's all experience.'

'Seakins,' said the professor, 'is very promising. He has just graduated and is one of our success stories.'

The Queen was a little put out that, despite her bright smile, serving the baeuf en croute Norman seemed determined not to catch her eye, and the same went for the poire belle-Helene. And it came to her that for some reason Norman was sulking, behaviour she had seldom come across except in children and the occasional cabinet minister. Subjects seldom sulked to the Queen as they were not entitled to, and once upon a time it would have taken them to the Tower.

A few years ago she would never have noticed what Norman was doing or anybody else either, and if she took note of it now it was because she knew more of people's feelings than she used to and could put herself in someone else's place. Though it still didn't explain why he was so put out.

'Books are wonderful, aren't they?' she said to the vicechancellor, who concurred.

'At the risk of sounding like a piece of steak,' she said, 'they tenderise one.'

He concurred again, though with no notion of what she was on about.

'I wonder,' she turned to her other neighbour,

'whether as professor of creative writing you would agree that if reading softens one up, writing does the reverse. To write you have to be tough, do you not?' Surprised to find himself discussing his own subject, the professor was momentarily at a loss. The Queen waited. 'Tell me,' she wanted to say, 'tell me I am right.' But the lord lieutenant was rising to wait upon her and the room shuffled to its feet. No one was going to tell her, she thought. Writing, like reading, was something she was going to have to do on her own.

Though not quite, and afterwards Norman is sent for, and the Queen, her lateness now proverbial but catered for in the schedule, spends half an hour being updated on his university career, including the circumstances that brought him to East Anglia in the first place. It is arranged that he will come to Sandringham the following day, where the Queen feels that now he has begun to write he may be in a position to assist her once again.

Between one day and the next, though, she sacked somebody else, and Sir Kevin came into his office in the morning to find his desk cleared. Though Norman's stint at the university had been advantageous Her Majesty did not like being deceived, and though the real culprit was the prime minister's special adviser Sir Kevin carried the can. Once it would have brought him to the block; these days it brought him a ticket back to New Zealand and an appointment as high commissioner. It was the block but it took longer.

SLIGHTLY TO her own surprise that year the Queen turned eighty. It was not a birthday that went unmarked and various celebrations were organised, some more to Her Majesty's liking than others, with her advisers tending to regard the birthday as just another opportunity to ingratiate the monarchy with the always fickle public.

It was not surprising, then, that the Queen decided to throw a party of her own and to assemble all those who had had the privilege of advising her over the years. This was in effect a party for the Privy Council, appointment to which is for life, thus making it a large and unwieldy body that in its entirety meets seldom and then only on occasions of some gravity. But there was nothing, thought the Queen, that would preclude her having them all to tea, and a serious tea at that, ham, tongue, mustard and cress, scones, cakes and even trifle.

Much preferable to dinner, she thought, and cosier altogether.

Nobody was told to dress up, though Her Majesty was as groomed and immaculate as she had been in the old days. But what a lot of advice she had had over the years, she thought, as she surveyed the crowded assembly; there were so many who had tendered it that they could only be accommodated in one of the grandest rooms in the palace, with the sumptuous tea laid out in two adjoining salons. She moved happily among her guests, unsupported by any other member of the royal family, who, though many of them were privy councillors, had not been invited. 'I see quite enough of them as it is,' she said, 'whereas I never see all of you and, short of my dying, there's no occasion when you're all likely to see each other. Do try the trifle. It's wicked.' Seldom had she been in such good spirits.

The prospect of a proper tea had fetched the privy councillors out in greater numbers than had been anticipated: dinner would have been a chore, whereas tea was a treat. There was such a crowd that chairs were in short supply, and there was a lot of running to and fro by the staff in order to get everybody seated, though this turned out to be part of the fun. Some sat on the usual gilt party chairs, but others found themselves ensconced on a priceless Louis XV bergere or a monogrammed hall chair brought in from the vestibule, with one former lord chancellor ending up perched on a little cork-topped stool brought down from a bathroom.

The Queen placidly surveyed all these goings-on, not quite on a throne but certainly on a chair larger than anyone else's. She had brought her tea in with her and sipped and chatted until at last everyone had made themselves comfortable.

'I know that I've been well advised over the years but I hadn't realised quite how numerously. What a crowd!'

'Perhaps, ma'am, we should all sing "Happy Birthday"!' said the prime minister, who was naturally sitting in the front row.

'Don't let's get carried away,' said Her Majesty. 'Though it is true one is eighty and this is a sort of birthday party. But quite what there is to celebrate I'm not sure. I suppose one of the few things to be said for it is that one has at least achieved an age at which one can die without people being shocked.'

There was polite laughter at this and the Queen herself smiled. 'I think', she said, 'that more shouts of "No, No" might be appropriate.'

So somebody obliged and there was more complacent laughter as the nation's most distinguished tasted the joys of being teased by the nation's most eminent.

'One has had, as you all know, a long reign. In fifty years and more I have gone through, I do not say seen off – (laughter) – 'ten prime ministers, six archbishops of Canterbury, eight speakers and, though you may not consider this a comparable statistic, fifty-three corgis – a life, as Lady Bracknell says, crowded with incident.'

The audience smiled comfortably, chuckling now and again. This was a bit like school, primary school anyway.

'And of course,' said the Queen, 'it goes on, not a week passing without something of interest, a scandal, a cover-up or even a war. And since this is one's birthday you must not even think of looking peeved' – (the prime minister was studying the ceiling and the home secretary the carpet) – 'for one has a long perspective and it was ever thus. At eighty things do not occur; they recur.'

'However, as some of you may know, I have always disliked waste. One not wholly mythical version of my character has me going round Buckingham Palace switching off the lights, the implication being that one is mean, though these days it could better be put down to an awareness of global warming. But disliking waste as I do puts me in mind of all the experiences I have had, many of them unique to me, the fruit of a lifetime in which one has been, if only as a spectator, very close to events. Most of that experience' – and Her Majesty tapped her immaculately coiffed head – 'most of it is up here. And one wouldn't want it to go to waste. So the question is, what happens to it?'

The prime minister opened his mouth as if to speak and indeed half rose from his chair.

'The question', said the Queen, 'was rhetorical.'

He sank back.

'As some of you may know, over the last few years I have become an avid reader. Books have enriched my life in a way that one could never have expected. But books can only take one so far and now I think it is time that from being a reader I become, or try to become, a writer.'

The prime minister was bobbing again and the Queen, reflecting that this was what generally happened to her with prime ministers, graciously yielded the floor.

'A book, Your Majesty. Oh yes, yes. Reminiscences of your childhood, ma'am, and the war, the bombing of the palace, your time in the WAAF.'

'The ATS,' corrected the Queen.

'The armed forces, whatever,' the prime minister galloped on. 'Then your marriage, the dramatic circumstances in which you learned you were Queen. It will be sensational. And,' he chortled, 'there's not much doubt that it will be a bestseller.'

'*The* bestseller,' trumped the home secretary. 'All over the world.'

'Ye-es,' said the Queen, 'only' – and she relished the moment – 'that isn't quite the kind of book one had in mind. That is a book, after all, that anyone can write and several people have – all of them, to my mind, tedious in the extreme. No, I was envisaging a book of a different sort.'

The prime minister, unsquashed, raised his eyebrows in polite interest. Maybe the old girl meant a travel book. They always sold well.

The Queen settled herself down. 'I was thinking of something more radical. More ... challenging.'

'Radical' and 'challenging' both being words that often tripped off the prime minister's tongue, he still felt no alarm.

'Have any of you read Proust?' asked the Queen of

the room.

Somebody deaf whispered 'Who?' and a few hands went up, the prime minister's not among them, and seeing this, one young member of the cabinet who had read Proust and was about to put his hand up didn't, because he thought it would do him no good at all to say so.

The Queen counted. 'Eight, nine – ten' – most of them, she noted, relics of much older cabinets. 'Well, that's something, though I'm hardly surprised. Had I asked Mr Macmillan's cabinet that question I'm sure a dozen hands would have gone up, including his. However that's hardly fair, as I hadn't read Proust at that time either.'

'I've read Trollope,' said a former foreign secretary.

'One is glad to hear it,' said the Queen, 'but Trollope is not Proust.' The home secretary, who had read neither, nodded sagely.

'Proust's is a long book, though, water-skiing permitting, you could get through it in the summer recess. At the end of the novel Marcel, who narrates it, looks back on a life that hasn't really amounted to much and resolves to redeem it by writing the novel which we have just in fact read, in the process unlocking some of the secrets of memory and remembrance.

'Now one's life, though one says it oneself, has, unlike Marcel's, amounted to a great deal, but like him I feel nevertheless that it needs redeeming by analysis and reflection.'

'Analysis?' said the prime minister.

'And reflection,' said the Queen.

Having thought of a joke that he knew would go down well in the House of Commons, the home secretary ventured on it here. 'Are we to assume that Your Majesty has decided to write this account because of something you read in a book, and a French book at that? Haw haw.'

There were one or two answering sniggers, but the Queen did not appear to notice that a joke had actually been made (as indeed it scarcely had). 'No, Home Secretary. But then books, as I'm sure you know, seldom prompt a course of action. Books generally just confirm you in what you have, perhaps unwittingly, decided to do already. You go to a book to have your convictions corroborated. A book, as it were, closes the book.'

Some of the councillors, long since out of government, were thinking that this was not the woman they remembered serving and were fascinated accordingly. But for the most part the gathering sat in uneasy silence, few of them having any idea what she was talking about. And the Queen knew it. 'You're puzzled,' she said, unperturbed, 'but I promise you, you do know this in your own sphere.'

Once again they were in school and she was their teacher. 'To inquire into the evidence for something on which you have already decided is the unacknowledged premise of every public inquiry, surely?'

The youngest minister laughed, then wished he hadn't. The prime minister wasn't laughing. If this was to be the tone of what the Queen was planning to write there was no telling what she was going to say. 'I still think you would do better just to tell your story, ma'am,' he said weakly.

'No,' said the Queen. 'I am not interested in facile reminiscence. It will, I hope, be something more thoughtful. Though when I say thoughtful I don't mean considerate. Joke.'

Nobody laughed and the smile on the prime minister's face had become a ghastly grin.

'Who knows,' said the Queen cheerfully, 'it might stray into literature.'

'I would have thought,' said the prime minister, 'that Your Majesty was above literature.'

'Above literature?' said the Queen. 'Who is above literature? You might as well say one was above humanity. But, as I say, my purpose is not primarily literary: analysis and reflection. What about those ten prime ministers?' She smiled brightly. 'There is much to reflect on there. One has seen the country go to war more times than I like to recall. That, too, bears thinking about.'

Still she smiled, though if anyone followed suit, it was the oldest ones who had the least to worry about.

'One has met and indeed entertained many visiting heads of state, some of them unspeakable crooks and blackguards and their wives not much better.' This at least raised some rueful nods.

'One has given one's white-gloved hand to hands that were steeped in blood and conversed politely with men who have personally slaughtered children. One has waded through excrement and gore; to be Queen, I have often thought, the one essential item of equipment a pair of thigh-length boots.

'One is often said to have a fund of common sense but that's another way of saying that one doesn't have much else and accordingly, perhaps, I have at the instance of my various governments been forced to participate if only passively in decisions I consider ill-advised and often shameful. Sometimes one has felt like a scented candle, sent in to perfume a regime, or aerate a policy, monarchy these days just a government-issue deodorant.

'I am the queen and head of the Commonwealth, but there have been many times in the last fifty years when that has made me feel not pride but shame. However' – and here she stood up – 'we must not lose our sense of priorities and this is a party after all, so before I continue shall we now have some champagne?'

The champagne was superb but, seeing that one of the pages doing the serving was Norman, the prime minister lost all taste for it and slipped along the corridor to the toilet, where he got on his mobile to the attorney general. The lawyer did much to reassure him, and fortified by his legal advice the prime minister was able to pass the message round the members of the cabinet, so that when in due course Her Majesty came back into the room it was a more resilient group that awaited her.

'We've been talking about what you said, ma'am,'

began the prime minister.

'All in good time,' said the Queen. 'One hasn't quite finished. I wouldn't want you to think that what I am planning to write and indeed have already started writing is some cheap, tell-tale, life-in-the-palace nonsense beloved of the tabloids. No. One has never written a book before but one hopes that it will' – she paused – 'transcend its circumstances and stand on its own, a tangential history of its times and, you'll perhaps be reassured to learn, far from exclusively to do with politics or the events of one's life. I'd like to talk about books, too, and people. But not gossip. I don't care for gossip. A roundabout book. I think it was E. M. Forster who said: "Tell all the truth but tell it slant, success in circuit lies." Or was it,' she asked the room, 'Emily Dickinson?'

Unsurprisingly, the room did not answer.

'But one mustn't talk about it or it will never get written.'

It was no comfort to the prime minister to reflect that whereas most people when claiming to want to write a book would never get it written, with the Queen and her terrible sense of duty it could be guaranteed that she would.

'Now, Prime Minister,' she turned to him gaily, 'you were saying?'

The prime minister rose. 'Respectful as we are of your intentions, ma'am' – the prime minister's tone was casual and friendly – 'I think I have to remind you that you are in a unique position.'

'I seldom forget it,' said the Queen. 'Go on.'

'The monarch has, I think I'm right in saying, never published a book.'

The Queen shook her finger at him, a gesture she remembered in the moment of making it that was a mannerism of Noel Coward's. 'That isn't quite true, Prime Minister. My ancestor Henry VIII, for instance, wrote a book. Against heresy. That is why one is still called Defender of the Faith. So, too, did my namesake Elizabeth I.'

The prime minister was about to protest.

'No, one knows it isn't the same, but my great-grand-mother Queen Victoria, she wrote a book also, *Leaves from a Highland Journal*, and a pretty tedious book it is, too, and so utterly without offence as to be almost unreadable. It's not a model one would want to follow. And then of course' – and the Queen looked hard at her first minister – 'there was my uncle the Duke of

Windsor. He wrote a book, *A King's Story*, the history of his marriage and subsequent adventures. If nothing else, that surely counts as a precedent?'

Furnished with the advice of the attorney general on this very point, the prime minister smiled and almost apologetically made his objection. 'Yes, ma'am, I agree, but the difference, surely, is that His Royal Highness wrote the book as Duke of Windsor. He could only write it because he had abdicated.'

'Oh, did I not say that?' said the Queen. 'But ... why do you think you're all here?'

THE UNCOMMON READER by Alan Bennett

Copyright © 2007 by Forelake Ltd

Simplified Chinese translation copyright © 2015 by Beijing Imaginist Time Culture Co. Ltd

Simplified Chinese edition arranged through Andrew Nurnberg Associates International Limited.

图书在版编目(CIP)数据

非普通读者：双语版：汉、英／(英)贝内特著；何宁译.

— 桂林：广西师范大学出版社，2015.5

ISBN 978-7-5495-6448-4

Ⅰ.①非… Ⅱ.①贝… ②何… Ⅲ.①长篇小说－英国－现代－汉、英

Ⅳ.①I561.45

中国版本图书馆CIP数据核字(2015)第055622号

广西师范大学出版社出版发行

　桂林市中华路22号 邮政编码：541001

　网址：www.bbtpress.com

出 版 人　何林夏

出 品 人　刘瑞琳

责任编辑　雷　韵

装帧设计　韩　凝

内文制作　韩　凝

全国新华书店经销

发行热线：010-64284815

北京盛源印刷有限公司

开本：787mm×1092mm　1/32

印张：7.5　字数：85千字

2015年5月第1版　2015年5月第1次印刷

定价：36.00元

如发现印装质量问题，影响阅读，请与印刷厂联系调换。